THE LONG RIFLE SEASON

MONGREL EMPIRE PRESS
NORMAN, OKLAHOMA, UNITED STATES OF AMERICA

2014

FIRST EDITION, 2014

The Long Rifle Season
© 2014 by James Murray

ISBN 978-0-9903204-1-8

Cover Image
the girl, the ravens, the hill © 2014 by Murv Jacob.

This is a work of fiction.
All of the characters, organizations and events portrayed in this novel are either products of the author's imagination or are used fictionally.

MONGREL EMPIRE PRESS
NORMAN, OK

ONLINE CATALOGUE: WWW.MONGRELEMPIRE.ORG

This publisher is a proud member of

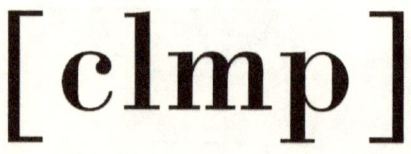

COUNCIL OF LITERARY MAGAZINES & PRESSES
www.clmp.org

Book Design: Mongrel Empire Press using iWork Pages

THE LONG RIFLE SEASON

Oklahoma Stories and Tales

JAMES MURRAY

CONTENTS

The Long Rifle Season   1

Amanda's Tale   7

Yard   11

Wewoka, 1974   13

Joe Bob's Tale   17

The Lord Works in Mysterious Ways   19

Painted Indians   23

A Short History   35

Carlos' Tale   37

Hell on Horses and Women   41

Fragment   57

Tharp's Tale   59

Pastor John's Tale   63

Hollis' Tale   67

Smoke   69

State Trooper   71

Randall's Tale   99

Rednecks In Conversation   103

Muskrat's Tale   109

June's Tale   113

Tim's Tale   117

La Harpe Amongst The Indians   123

High Plains, May 1868   133

for the cowboys and indians

THE LONG RIFLE SEASON

There is nary a crossroads or clearing in Cherokee County that hasn't been watered by blood at one time or another. As soon as the Tearful Trail emptied its diaspora into these woodlands, the Cherokees started erasing the slateboards with blood feuds and secret society assassinations. Bowie knives found jugular veins and musketeer ambuscades emptied saddles along deer trails. When the accounts finally settled, it was civil war time. Cherokee and Mvskoke and Missouri guerrilla and Texas cavalry and bound African shot and hacked and slashed and burnt against Kansas Jayhawker and union infantry and blue-uniformed freedmen. Stand Watie and his men were the last to leave the grey war path and the snow and rain comforted the traces of common graves and homesteads burnt to ashes.

But the blood kept flowing like old Snake Creek, drying up into shallow ponds in the summer sun of occasional prosperity and washing up over the banks in the spring hard rain times. There were outlaws like Ned

Christie, a man who had drawn his share of draughts. He Winchestered a U.S. Marshal in '78 then spent the next decade fortified in the Cookson Hills, putting bullets into the men they sent to capture him. Finally, they brought in a mule-drawn artillery piece from Fort Smith and Ned died, bleeding into the ground.

Two dirt farmers sat drinking away on Tahlequah's main street in '09. They squabbled over a hog and one fella drew his pistol but the other fella was faster with his Bowie knife. The knife cleaved one ol boy's skull at the same time the .44-.40 round struck nothing but hard-packed earth.

At the old Goingsnake courthouse in '80, a half-breed cowboy was on trial for murdering a romantic rival. When the jury foreman said "Guilty," the cowboy's cousin stood up from his seat and tossed the defendant a Colt SAA and drew two more of his own. Pistols thundered and flashed, and when the smoke cleared, they carried four men dead out of the courthouse and five more wounded. Both cowboys and two Cherokee Nation marshals were dust-biters that day.

Right up to 1900, wild indians from the prairie would ride east to the green hills on pony-thieving jaunts. They'd swoop through the Nation on full-moon summer nights collecting brood mares and range horses and then ride gut-busting back west while a posse formed. But it was a tough way to get horses and got too expensive. Posses made up of full-bloods, white outlaws and half-breed cowboys had grain-fed horses and repeating rifles. Many an indian never returned to the flat land.

All this while neighbors were killing neighbors over corn-liquor grudges or missing steers and strangers were killing neighbors over pretty daughters or rumors of hoarded silver and neighbors were killing strangers over reasons of their own.

Cherokee Bill wasn't much Cherokee and his mama didn't name him Bill but he murdered and raped and fed the coyotes along Spring Creek with his victims. His weakness was choc-houses and the Nation marshals finally got him at the cost of one of their own. When they watched him swing from the gallows they spat and said his damned hide wasn't worth the good man they lost to catch him.

Jesse James and Belle Starr trusted in Tahlequah but they had the good sense to steal somewhere else where everything wasn't already being stolen and where Winchesters and Remingtons weren't tied to every saddle. While that pair was holed up dreaming of Missouri banks and Tennessee walking horses, old men were killing young men at rifle distance and young men were killing old men with pistols and middle-aged men were killing old men and young men with whatever their hands fell upon when tempers lost in drink and drudgery broke like hickory sticks with pop and crash.

And that pretty Floyd boy was a live wire. He slipped farm wives hundred-dollar bills for breakfast from Joplin to Eufaula and hid out in the country of the Cookson Hills. On the old highway running from Cherokee County to west of the river, he crashed his Ford and went Thompson gun to Winchester 97 with a half-dozen lawmen. They filled his car with buckshot but somehow he got away to charge another bank.

The Cherokee counties were dry for decades but there was no shortage of sundry spirits. Blood and sour mash admixtures spilled across dirt roads and dripped into creek beds. Money owed and squandered gambling was paid back in wet holler shotgunnings. Beer-drunk indians and whiskey-drunk cowboys practicing moving-picture pistol-tricks took the tops of their own heads off with single-action .45s and put .38-.44 bullets through the spines of the their second cousins.

I pull up at the public gun range on Pryor Creek and take the O3-A3 Springfield and a handful of stripper clips out from behind the seat of the truck. It's a clear late-summer morning with endless blue sky stretching in every direction. I take the rifle out of its case and head down the embankment and set up targets (beer cans) around the steep creek bank. I pace off a hundred steps and sit down cross-legged next to a short pine tree. I go into a hasty loop firing position with my left arm supporting the rifle that is pressed into my right shoulder. I charge the rifle with my right hand and drop the clip. Closing the bolt, I look through the sights at my targets. I squeeze the trigger and hit the first can—clods of earth fly from the backstop. Then I miss the second, and third (trigger happy) and connect again with the fourth and fifth. I leave the bolt open and sit for a moment with my rifle in my lap. An eighteen-wheeler speeds past shifting gears on the state highway. Somewhere above, a plane drones on. I pick up the empty brass.

The years haven't slackened the blood springs of Cherokee County. Every winter some drunk knocks over a space heater, incinerating the family rattletrap mobile home around sleeping daughters and every summer some farm boy rolls his granddad's tractor over on himself. Every spring, a carload of teenagers cheap-drunk on sloe gin heavy-metals straight through a hairpin curve, smashing into standing hardwood at seventy miles per hour. Every fall, a deer hunter manages to simultaneously fall out of a tree stand and shoot himself. When it is real cold, chainsaws buck out of knotty red oak and into the skulls of men who had never owned a safety helmet. When it is real hot, grandpas and toddlers drown in ponds and creeks and lakes. The seasonal traditions still exist here, life-taking in their regularity.

I had always been told when young that, "When you go east of the river you take a gun." Which was sensible enough advice. I'm sure my Dad, in telling me this, was worried about wild indians but it soon became apparent when I was old enough to motor over the bridge that the cowboys (crazy, drunk, armed) were far more dangerous. I myself am Scots-Irish cowboy by heritage, casually brutal, dog-loving, with innate desires to kill large mammals and get intoxicated. And the cowboys still shoot each other with some regularity. Sam deer-snuck into his ex-wife's trailer and found her sleeping with a guy with a beard. He put a .357 into the sleeping man's head. T. Barnes killed two men (on separate occasions) with a pool cue and then got shot in the face by a hippie outside the store in Peggs. Randall was coming back from feeding his cattle one night and found three men burglarizing his trailer. He shot all three of them with his .243 varminter. Barrett put up a sign on his gate that read, "I don't give a shit who you are, if you cross this fence I will shoot you." I guess he meant it—the first two state troopers who tried to serve the felony warrant were met with inaccurate .223 fire that somehow managed to get both of their widows handed a flag.

The indians, though not as violent, are more accident-prone. They specialize in propane explosions and collisions with eighteen-wheelers. They get tangled in discarded fishing line and drown while noodling catfish. They are struck by lightning in the goat pen and bitten by rattlesnakes while on coonhunting jaunts.

As always, it is the deer and coyote that offer up the most blood to the tree and grass roots. We still pay attention to the animals here and we treat them like our own. We shoot them out of deep love and faithful hatred. We run over them in trucks like they were children in the city. We notice their tracks in the mud and wet snow and dip our hands into their carcasses and glory in their blood and fur stuck staining our arms and clothes.

I sat and soaked up the sun with the old Springfield across my knees. It is a wonderful rifle. More dependable than the man who operated it. All it needs is bullets. When I lived in the city and worked construction jobs, more than once I had been sitting around bullshitting with the guys and, almost sheepish, they'd turn to the wars they had missed. They doubted themselves: could they do it? Could they kill someone? In Cherokee County, there is no such angst. We are a county of killers; deer or men could end the same way. You use the sights, squeeze the trigger. The rifle does the rest. I hadn't shot anyone, yet. But I was acculturated into the knowledge that rural Scots-Irish Okie males share, that someday we would be forced to kill. The knowledge is as present as the smell of fresh cut hay. It drifts away but always returns. It is acknowledged and sometimes spoken. It is why you wanted a .45 or .357 instead of a 9 millimeter. "Cause when you shoot someone you want to kill them." My Dad never said much but what he said was sensible.

Somebody said something about colonial wars and mental disorders? It never ended. The indians have alcoholism and diabetes. The cowboys have alcoholism and heart disease. The drugs and gunpowder we all share. A continuation of the frontier by other means.

AMANDA'S TALE

Why does everyone always claim to be part Cherokee? No one ever claims that they are part Hopi or Sac and Fox. It's always that they had a full-blood grandma who was a Cherokee princess. I've studied Cherokee history for years and I have an M.A. in Native Studies and I'm here to tell you: there were no Cherokee princesses. Where that comes from I don't know. For some reason, white people want to be Cherokee, they don't want to be Salish or Choctaw.

I guess for one reason it's believable. There are a lot of white people with Cherokee Nation CDIB cards. When you go to the indian hospital or free clinic that's what you see, white people waiting to be seen by a doctor. That's what pisses native people off. Hell, it pisses me off! But then I take my son to the ER when he has a fever and I see all these white people in line in front of us. And I look at my son and realize he looks white, too. I mean he's Cherokee but you would never know to look at him. He's at least a quarter but he takes after his father, blonde hair and blue eyes. So is he a whiteboy to the native people in line behind him? I guess so. It's so crazy you can't make sense of it. I don't even know who's Cherokee and I'm supposed to be an expert on this shit.

When I was a little girl everyone knew who was an indian. It was obvious. I was obviously an indian—dark skin, dark hair, dark eyes. Like my aunts and uncles. Like my Mom I guess but I never really knew her. My Grandma was my Mom, that's who raised me. My Mom just wanted to drink and do drugs and she's dead now. I think the Hep C killed her. My real Dad is still alive but I have never talked to him. He's part indian too, 1/4 Creek I think. So I grew up real indian and real poor. Sometimes I think those things go together, that you have to be real poor to be a real indian. But I hate thinking like that.

My Grandma was a real indian, a full-blood, very poor and very traditional. She smoked the four corners of the house each morning and was very superstitious, always warning us about ghosts and bad witches and little people and things. As a girl I was scared all the time. Scared of everything. And always embarrassed in front of white people. I thought all white people were rich.

When I got out of high school, I was so tired of being a poor embarrassed indian girl I didn't know what to do. So I joined the army. In basic training I destroyed my knee, just destroyed it. In retrospect maybe that's for the best. That was 1990, and the next year we invaded Iraq. So I missed out on all that. The army sent me home. I wasn't that thrilled to be back in Oklahoma. It was a very difficult time for me. I had a lot of anger and no where to direct it. This is Sequoyah County, 1992 and 3. Nothing to do but get drunk. Minimum wage jobs, white boyfriends, indian boyfriends, all of them ignorant and jealous and potentially violent. It's easy to get trapped in that madness for life. I know, I've seen it happen many times. I guess that's what happened to my Mom.

I still drink too much sometimes but somehow I got out. Started taking college classes and realized I could be smart. I got my degree and moved to Tahlequah where Cherokee history drips off the trees like rain and got a good job at the Nation. Along the way I got married, had a son, got divorced, got re-married and divorced again and well, you know the story.

YARD

A wheelbarrow on its side with tire deflated, crushed flat beer cans, spent .223 shells, empty chainsaw oil containers, a weathered lariat coil snaking without purpose, shredded dog food sacks, rotting two-by-fours, decomposing Wal-Mart sacks, a bicycle tire, rusting horse shoes, pallets not stacked but thrown one upon the other, a come-a-long lying handle-pointed-up atop a red oak stump, a Eufaula newspaper (never read), its pages yellowing together from spring rain; raccoon bones, a woman's cowboy boot, a molding straw bale, losing lottery tickets, crushed, wadded, and ripped apart Marlboro 100 boxes; fifty feet of watering hose, a Ford F-250 4 x 4 truck with window down and hood up, a shattered rain gauge, Skoal can lids, an old propane refrigerator, two calico cats, a broken axe handle, Braum's milk crates, a flattened pair of sunglasses, a leather belt minus the buckle, bags of concrete solidified from morning dew, Mason jar rings.

House

Ruger Mini-14 with three D-cell flashlight batteries taped to barrel end, feed sacks overflowing with beer cans, empty Harbor Pizza boxes, a sleeping pit bull, four camo ball caps, empty thirty-can beer cases, *Hustler* magazines, coffee cans packed with cigarette butts, a pile of Carhartt clothing, encrusted dishes, two televisions (neither working), army surplus ammo cans, unopened utility bills, an electric space heater, a double bed with polyester Confederate flag quilt wadded to one side, fly strips thumbtacked to ceiling, empty bourbon bottles.

Kitchen

Empty jelly jars, molded bread still in wrapper, shredded lunchmeat packs, propane two-burner camp stove atop peeled linoleum next to sink, a metal bucket containing anhydrous ammonia, Coleman lantern fluid in a can, mixing bowls full of Sudafed and Contac cold pills.

Driveway

The McIntosh County Sheriff's Department SWAT team getting out of a van.

WEWOKA, 1974

In official terms, Willie Lena was Chief of the Seminole Tallahassee town but for all practical purposes he was town chief of Wewoka. From early in the morning to late at night, cars and trucks were pulling into his driveway or parking in his yard. The people came to borrow small sums of money or to pay back the same. Or they were wishing to acquire indian medicine and maybe have Willie conjure for them. Some came asking advice in personal matters or to see if Willie would mediate in a dispute. His visitors were Seminole or Creek mostly, but in recent years, white people had been coming too. They wanted to buy one of his drawings or hand-made crafts. Or, they were anthropologists or linguists wanting explanations of obscure Mvskoke pronunciation or a bit of what they called "oral tradition," to fit into a thesis.

Willie welcomed everyone with good humor and the more than occasional ribald joke. He didn't work. This was his job. He did it every day.

The Creek boy had waited a long time to see him, smoking cigarettes under a shade tree. He was finally ushered into the house where Willie sat, holding court in a rocking chair, a stained Stetson upon his head, his hands busy carving a piece of cane with a jackknife. Willie like the boy immediately. There was a little bit of black Creek in him, Willie thought, and some white, too. He had a seriousness of purpose that Willie immediately read. The boy wanted stickball medicine. "I can do that," Willie told him, "But there's a better way if you have the courage."

"OK. What is it?"

"There's an old way to become the best stickball player." Willie sat his cane and knife on a table, his eyes grew bright. "When I was a young man, your age maybe, I was the best stickball player around. But then in 1934, I got stabbed in the leg and my stickball days were over."

"How did you become the best?"

"The old way. My uncle told me. It works."

"What is it?"

Willie looked at the boy intently. "Sonny," he said, "You know how to make the horned owl call?"

The boy shook his head. Willie cupped his hands around his mouth and demonstrated the call, "*Whoo-ah. Whoo-ah. Woo-ah.*"

"I tell you what you do—take your stickball sticks and go to where the horned owl lives. A place where a whole lotta trees meets a pasture is a good place. Take off your clothes and sit down and make the horned owl call. That horned owl will hear it and will make him mad. He's gonna wanna come fight cause you're mocking him. When he comes down—fight him with your sticks. And be ready to put up a good fight cause that horned owl is pretty mean. That's what you do to be the best stickball player."

Willie was smiling broadly. He could see the skepticism in the boy's face. Willie laughed out loud and unsnapped the pearl snaps on his cowboy shirt. He pulled the shirt open. The boy's eyes widened. Even after fifty years, the talon scars that criss-crossed Willie's chest were unmistakable.

JOE BOB'S TALE

At one time, I was ranked third in the world. Bull riding. There's nothing like it. I loved every minute. The pain you learn to deal with or you get out. That's why you do drugs. I'd buy an 8-ball of speed and an 8-ball of cocaine and mix it all together. That's what it takes to kill the pain and keep you going. I drove from Moody, Oklahoma to the Detroit Silverdome one time. There and back, straight through. Was only in Detroit three hours. Got there, registered, rode a bull and got bucked off. Disqualified. I just drove back to Oklahoma doing lines and drinking beer the whole way. That was like a forty-hour sprint. When I was high-rollin, I wouldn't even bother sleeping with one woman. If I couldn't take two home I'd just blow it off and keep drinking. Women love bull riders. I'd be so banged up from bulls and so fucked up from the shit I couldn't even fuck them sometimes. I'd just bring em back to the hotel and watch em go at it.

It's a crazy life. Like being a rock star, but your life is on the line. I don't care how banged up and hurt you are or how much drugs you are on. When you climb into the chute and get on a bull's back you get an adrenaline rush that cuts through everything. It's unbelievable. That's why guys can't stop. It feels too good. There's no replacement. It makes your ears ring. You'll go bankrupt and keep riding bulls. Watch your wife walk away with the kids and keep riding bulls. Piss blood every day for months and keep riding bulls. Watch the bank take your house and keep riding bulls. Some guys, the smart ones probably, snap at some point and get spooked and can't do it anymore. That's the smart way out. But I'm straight-up Oklahoma cowboy and I never claimed to be smart. I went out the hard way. In Billings, a bull threw me and I hit the dirt face first and he jumped and landed on my back. Spinal fracture at L5. I'll never walk again.

It's tough, no doubt, but I ain't gonna get those legs back. I just have to deal with. It was hard on my Dad, too —he got me into the business and he blamed himself. Me being crippled shortened his life, I'm sure. When he was dying he told me was sorry and apologized and I can't lie, I cried like a baby. That's the first time I really thought it was all a mistake. I got depressed real bad. Had my sister come over and take my pistols cause honest to god I didn't trust myself to be around them. But I got over it. You can't let life eat you up with what you've lost or what you don't have. There's too many things to live for.

THE LORD WORKS
IN MYSTERIOUS WAYS

Not that Floyd had ever paid much attention to superior authority before, but when the Lord told him to steal his neighbor Harold's truck and drive into Tahlequah and murder his ex-wife, he listened. He had long suspected his ex was host to demonic spirits. Of course, he would need Harold's truck. Floyd's own Chevy was listing on under-inflated tires and wouldn't start. And even if it had started, there was not enough gas in the tank to drive into Quah. Floyd was broke, too, which precluded the purchase of gasoline. And even if he had money, he had recently written both of the stores in Peggs hot checks. So he was in no way anxious to make an appearance in either establishment.

Stealing Harold's truck would have been easier if Floyd had a firearm, but the pawnshop in Locust Grove was holding both his rifle and shotgun in lieu of repayment on a high-interest loan. Floyd did, however, have a compound bow and a clutch of arrows. He counted out three practice points and two broad heads. Then he finished his can of Busch beer and pulled on his army surplus camo field jacket and walked over to Harold's house.

Harold was examining his telephone bill for errors of commission when he saw Floyd in his front yard taking up an archery stance and aiming a bow and arrow at his house. "What the hell is that fool doing?" he asked his wife and walked out on the porch.

"I ain't playin around!" Floyd shouted at his neighbor, "I'se stealin your truck! Throw your keys out here!"

"What?"

"I'se stealin your truck!"

"The hell you are."

"Doan make me stick you wit an arrow Harold! Throw your keys out!"

"My goodness," Harold's wife said from within the house, "Is he serious?"

"I believe he is," replied Harold as he walked back inside the house. Harold's first instinct was to pick up the Ruger .357 magnum off of the coffee table and just shoot his idiotic neighbor. But then he reflected: his truck had two-hundred thirty-one thousand miles on the odometer and the front end was badly out of line and yet it remained fully insured. What the hell, thought Harold, and he threw his keys out in the front yard. As Floyd climbed in the truck and started it up, Harold dialed the Oklahoma Highway Patrol non-emergency number. "A blithering idiot named Floyd Alberty jus stole my truck and it looks like he's turning south on 82 headin towards Tahlequah." He told the dispatcher his truck's make model and color and went back to his phone bill.

Within minutes an OHP trooper spotted the stolen truck and was pursuing it at a high rate of speed. Floyd, however, had no intentions of pulling over. He was not about to let lights and sirens interfere with the task given him by God. But the truck's transmission was apparently outside the realm of holy writ—it began downshifting and sliding through the gears and brought the truck to a sputtering halt on a long curving incline. Grabbing his bow and arrows, he leapt out of the truck and dashed into the heavily-brushed forest. The OHP trooper had been well-schooled: "Never follow anyone into the woods of Cherokee County," so he radioed for backup and a tracking dog and a tactical team as Floyd blundered and crashed through the leaves and underbrush.

Floyd Alberty was not a man anyone would consider lucky nor was he even mildly fortunate. But God had a plan for him and, as they say, the Lord looks after his own. And so, with obvious foresight, the Lord had dispatched Floyd on his criminal spree on the last day of Oklahoma's generous deer season. Within an hour of entering the woods, Floyd stumbled onto a pair of hunters, both with ATVs and scoped hunting rifles. He held them at arrow-point and took both rifles and the nicest of the ATVs. Providence held sway for Floyd—most locals would have shot him outright, but the hunters were dentists from Tulsa. Seized by terror and surprise, they meekly acquiesced.

Floyd roared off on the stolen ATV and steered the machine back to highway 82 south. Up the embankment and onto the pavement he rode, with one rifle slung on his back and the other strapped to the ATV. OHP troopers, county deputies, and Cherokee Nation marshals from a thirty-mile radius had arrived on the scene and he was quickly spotted driving down the highway's shoulder with the ATV's speed maxed out. Floyd looked behind him and saw he was being chased by almost a dozen black and white squad cars, all in a line. He drove off the highway and rolled through tall grass, wishing he had a pair of wire cutters so he could cut through barbed fences and ride the ATV overland to Quah. But no wire cutters did he have. With the authorities now closing in on him from all directions, he stopped the ATV and unslung the rifle from his back.

"Don't do it!" He could hear them shouting, "Put the gun down!" But Floyd was obeying a higher authority and he pressed the rifle's butt into his shoulder and jerked the trigger. Through the rifle's scope, he saw a black and white's windshield shatter and three OHP troopers firing at him simultaneously. The .223 bullets destroyed his left kidney and shattered his right kneecap and sliced through the fat around his waist and blew off his left pinkie finger.

They gave him a nice ride in the medical helicopter to Tulsa where they patched him up and, many weeks later, sent him back to the county jail in Tahlequah. There, he attempted to start a Bible study group but no one was interested.

PAINTED INDIANS

I hadn't seen Dave in a couple of years and I remembered the last time well—a 4th of July at Roxie's on the river. A forest fire up the cliff was raging and dropping burning embers all over the place. Shit-faced college girls in bikinis and cut-offs stumbled about and R. Crouch was playing outside, super *wa-wa-ing* on a Stratocaster. The volunteer fire department showed up to put out the small fires caused by the dropping embers and some crazy middle-aged drunk bitches were flashing them tits and ass. The whole scene was vaguely reminiscent of *Apocalypse Now*, and in the middle of it stood my pal and sometime running-buddy, Dave Pony-Stealer, a painter and intellectual with a rich Cherokee mom and a long-dead Comanche father. Dave was standing amidst the chaos shooting off bottle rockets without the aid of a bottle—just lighting them with a cigarette and tossing them forward to launch erratically into the air. I remember the look of drunken boyish bliss on Dave's face. He's a wild indian, I remember thinking, and this is as close as he'll ever get to shooting a Trapdoor Springfield at the 10th Cavalry. After a while, the fire department drove off and Dave scored several direct hits on their tanker truck with his bottle rockets, celebrating each time like he had just downed a buffalo.

Then Dave dropped off the face of the earth. I heard that he had gotten married again and moved to Norman.

A year later, I ran into him on the deck of a coffeeshop on main street. Dave and I are much alike: we were born within days of each other in the summer of 1969 and we are about the same size, although Dave's gut is expanding faster than my own. And we share many of the same interests: women, art, 19th century combat, the last year of the Third Reich, etc. On this occasion, our unplanned reunion, we were dressed as though our common mother had dressed her little (bad) boys in matching outfits of camo and caps and cowboy shirts. It was slightly embarrassing.

A few minutes into our conversation, I learned the truth about Dave's whereabouts and current situation: he had walked out on his wife in Norman and was back living with his sister in Tahlequah. "I only made two mistakes when I left," he told me, "I forgot the keys to the Lincoln and my checkbook." I nodded in sympathy and then he reconsidered. "Well, I guess I made another mistake. Before I left I took a framing hammer and smashed every object of value in the house." That was sick and wrong but I understood perfectly. Dave was deeply atavistic and he couldn't help himself; his DNA told him, "leave nothing for the enemy."

We ordered beers and Dave continued, "I just couldn't get anything done in Norman," he said, "Her kids were always having to be taken here or there or somewhere and I just can't deal with the constant motion that gets you nowhere." Dave paused and gulped some beer. "And there's only one way I can paint and I know it—drink from 6PM to midnight, paint all night and crash at dawn. Man, it's hard to do that with a wife who has two kids. Again, I sympathized, and Dave went on.

"I kept getting commissions that I couldn't do. I'd get 3K up front and immediately spend the money and never do the painting. Then, I'd have to give the money back. I've already spent 14k not painting this year. A fucking nightmare. Norman sucks, Tahlequah is really the only place I can work. It's the bitch succubus of Indian Territory."

I agreed there was something in the air or water locally that made one bend towards criminality and artistic expression. It was a *thing*, weird and unknowable but certainly extant.

Dave took another drink. "And then of course she went total head-case. Everything turned into a blood feud. Like, do you want Mexican or Chinese and suddenly were debating like we're in the Roman Senate and trying to decide whether or not to invade Gaul. I just can't take it. All I want to do is paint and drink and read books. That's all I care about, man."

"Yeah, yeah," I replied.

The day was warm, the earth beginning to tilt toward sun, and as I filled Dave in on my recent exploits and failures, a hotrod '55 Chevy screeched to a halt on the street in front of us. Charles Mingus blasted from the speakers and my adopted uncle leapt from the car. A big Cherokee in his early 60s, Fred Bear was an award-winning artist and book illustrator and complete wildman. Fred walked up on the deck pointing his finger at us and feigning disbelief.

"You two," he said, "You two sorry scoundrels."

Fred was (strangely?) dressed almost exactly as Dave and I; he clutched an oversized Sharpie in one hand and a vintage thermos in the other. Sweat poured from him in waves and I suspected he had gone home for lunch and made coffee then liberally sprinkled the black drink with mescaline.

Heavy and dripping though he was, he shuffle-strutted towards us like Brando in a '50s biker flick, "Jesus christ staggering on a crooked crutch," he said and dropped his bulk into a chair next to us, "I'm a goddamn anarchist and there oughtta be a law against you two being anywhere near each other!"

Dave and I laughed and I shut up and let the two Indian painters gossip and play catch-up.

Some hippie girls came out of the café to smoke and sat at a table near us. So much sweat was coming off Fred that it was pooling under the chair he sat in. He shifted in his chair and half-faced the girls. Oh no, I thought, the drugs are kicking in—there is no telling what he might say.

"Do you have any idea," Fred addressed the girls, "Who these pirates of the Cherokee are?" He pointed at Dave and I and the girls shrugged politely. Fred told them, "That's Josh Pike, he's a writer. He's one of these anti-civilization people."

I was wishing I could crawl under the table to hide when Fred pointed at Dave, "And that big Indian he's running with is Dave Pony-Stealer. A historical painter with an epic thirst for Irish beer and white women. You girls aren't safe anywhere near these guys!"

"No no no," I interrupted, laughing, "I'm harmless. It's Dave you gotta worry about."

"Shit," Dave shrugged, "I've got a domestic violence conviction so I can't even own firearms." He giggled, amusing himself.

The hippie girls stared at us with equal parts shock, disgust, and awe. I attempted damage control, "We're just kidding," I said, "We're just artists kidding around."

"Bull-shit!" Fred bellowed. "You trying to tell me you ain't the reincarnation of some head-takin Highlander?" Dave started laughing and so did I but Fred remained deeply serious. "I got to go paint a badger," he said and got up and left without another word.

Several hours later, Dave and I were ordering beers at the brand new pseudo-Irish pub on Tahlequah's main street when a drunk college girl careened into me then ricocheted into Dave, who caught her by the arms. "My shorts are falling down," she said, "You can see my thong." She stepped away and bent over, her round white ass on display with a black thong running between her cheeks. "Nice ass," Dave said.

"Thanks, man."

My God, I thought, this girl has no idea what she is playing with.

"My shorts keep falling down," she told Dave, "They are too loose."

Dave unbuckled his belt and pulled it out of his camo shorts. "Here you go," he said, "You can have mine."

"Thanks, Dude!" She threaded the belt into her cut-offs and asked,""What's your name?"

"David Pony-Stealer."

"Wut? Pony-Stealer?"

"Yes."

"You an indian?"

"Yes. Cherokee and Comanche."

"I thought you were a Mexican or something."

"Not at all."

"Oh shit!" The girl tried to fasten the belt and it was much too large. "Your belt don't fit, Dude." Dave held onto the girl's hip and slowly extracted the belt from her cut-offs. "You got a knife, Chooch?" I handed him one. Dave laid the belt down on the bar and stabbed into it then handed it back to her. "Don't lose my belt," he told her, "I'll need it later to tie you to your bedpost."

"HAHAHA!" She cackled and moved off.

We had another beer (Dave usually drank three to my one) and as usual we talked about the Little Big Horn. "It's all bullshit," Dave said, "Custer is the big villain and Crazy Horse the big hero. Do you know how Crazy Horse became heap big chief?"

I knew. "By killing Pawnee," I said.

"Yeah, Chooch, Crazy Horse killed way more indians than Custer ever did!"

"Oh, yeah. Any attempt to construct a liberal analysis of American history is doomed to failure. There is nothing liberal about it. It's like cats trying to understand dogs."

"Yeah, bro. But they try like fuck!"

"Oh I know, Dave—"

"It's like these fucking Cherokees. Trail of Tears this and Trail of Tears that. It's so tiring and old."

"The indian as victim is acceptable and not threatening," I opined. "The indian as aggressor is too scary for the masses. The Cherokee Nation, Inc. doesn't want to deal with that shit."

"Fuck the CN," Dave motioned to the bartender, "Go up there and look in their offices, it's just a bunch of white people with CDIB cards." Dave washed down the remaining beer in his glass and put his hand on my shoulder, "But I do hope they accept my bid for the casino mural. I could use the 40K."

We laughed and Dave threw his credit card on the bar and ordered two whiskey shots. The bourbon burned my throat and felt good and warm in my stomach. Dave launched into a long meandering examination of his troubles with women. I listened and silently compared/contrasted our positions vis-á-vis the female gender. I mostly like women whereas Dave mostly did not. He hung out with women so he could sleep with them and I slept with them so they would let me hang out. We represented the two basic types of womanizing macho artists. I was reminded of the Lou Reed line, "It's a boring macho trip, but I'm the type that fascinates." And, luckily, our tastes were different as well. Dave went for the petit blondes every time whereas I liked the slightly rounded brunettes and redheads.

He finally wound down and I told him I had gone to a party a few days before and met a little twenty-four year-old that I was kind of crushing on. "We have nothing in common and I'm way too old for her but we kind of hit it off," I told him.

"Is she hot?"

"Of course."

"Is she an idiot?"

"No, she seemed smart enough. Witty. Completely uneducated but they all are."

"Hey man," Dave told me, "Education's way-overrated. I mean—do you actually talk to your women?"

"Not really." I shrugged in admission.

"Then what does it matter if she's educated or not?"

"Good point Dave. I knew I could rely on you to talk me into it."

"Go for it man. Shit. Last year I cheated on my wife with a twenty-two year-old OU grad student."

"Was it good?"

"I was so drunk the whole time I can't even remember the details. But my point is, she was uneducated too. She's getting an M.A. in anthropology and I had to explain to her how to use a bibliography."

"What are they teaching these kids?"

"Nothing. They just take their money and push them through."

"Yeah," I said, "I see it every day. One day I was hanging out at Fred's studio and these college kids come in and Fred starts questioning them and the boy says he's studying 'Marketing,' and Fred asks, 'why?' and the kid says so he could add value to commodities. We howled at that one. Fred laughed so hard he fell in the floor and rolled around. I thought he was going to have a heart attack."

Dave laughed and I started planning my escape from the bar. He was jovial enough now but I knew that could change instantly. After six or eight beers, if things went bad, it would take several deputies to subdue him. But after fifteen or twenty beers it might take a SWAT team and stun grenades. I wanted no part of that. The college girl with the loose shorts wandered back by and Dave put his arm around her and whispered in her ear. She giggled and Dave winked at me. I saluted him by touching the bill of my cap and walked out of the bar and drove home through the ancient Cherokee forest painted dark and green for a wet summer.

Weeks later, Dave's mother called me and told me that Dave had "fallen" out of the Irish pub's second floor deck and nearly killed himself. She didn't describe his injuries exactly but she put him on the line to speak with me briefly. Slurring his words, Dave said he would like to see me and that he was doing OK. "I'm just resting a lot," he told me, "Reading my Bible and Toland's biography of Hitler." I promised to come see him and we hung up.

A couple of weeks later, I went to see him at his mother's upscale house on the lake. Dave's left arm was immobilized and his head was still swollen and he had a cast on his left ankle. Dave's Mom brought us coffee and we sat chatting. "Mom," Dave said, "Do you mind if Josh and I have a moment alone?" She didn't mind and left the room. Dave and I sat looking at each other. He sighed deeply. "I didn't fall," he said.

"You didn't fall?"

"I was pushed."

"Pushed?"

"Yes. By an invisible white owl."

"What?" I sat forward in shock.

"That's right bro—pushed."

"If it was invisible how do you know it was a white owl?"

"Dude, I'm indian. We know this shit."

"Oh my god Dave . . ."

"There's shit on me," Dave said, "I've been smoked."

"Smoked?"

"That's right bro—smoked."

"Who would smoke you?"

"Some jealous indian artist."

I sat back, "You think so?"

"I know it. These Cherokees are a very jealous people. They see someone like me who's half-Comanche being successful and they can't take it. If I was half-white they would love me but no—they just can't take it. They will smoke your ass bro."

"Shit."

"You know it's true."

"Christ," I shook my head.

"Hey man," Dave leaned forward and took a sip of Coke through a straw, "You know a *tsgili*?"

"What?" I feigned surprise, "Why you askin' a *unega* bout *tsgilis*?"

"Dude, I grew up southern Babtist."

"So did I, Dave."

"But you know the full-bloods."

"Bullshit, I know three or four maybe."

"You think like a full-blood."

"Like a full-blood Scot maybe."

"Josh, man c'mon. I'm all fucked up layin here helpless with smoke on me. I'm asking for help here and all you can do is fuck with me in my time of need. C'mon."

"OK. OK."

"You gotta take me to the *tsgili* man."

"OK."

I called the old man and set up an appointment and when Dave could drive, we met outside the coffee shop in Tahlequah. He got in my truck and we drove up into the hills. I knew where the old man lived; I had been out there several times to attend sweat lodges. Where the paved road curved, we went straight onto gravel.When we pulled up in the driveway, I saw that nothing had changed: dogs roamed in a pack and dozens of vehicles, mostly trucks and late model luxury sedans, sat parked among weeds and piles of construction materials.

Stiff and slow, Dave got out of my truck and we walked up to the porch. "He's in there wit someone," an old woman told us so we sat on benches on the porch and chatted about the mild weather. A Cherokee woman about thirty years old came out of the house and handed us cups of coffee. She was wearing an unmarked black baseball cap and an ancient Merle Haggard concert t-shirt with the sleeves cut off to show "Red Power," "Native Pride" and prison tattoos marking her arms from shoulder to wrist. "Which a you is goin in?" she asked and I pointed at Dave. She nodded. "He said to go on in." Dave patted my shoulder for encouragement, sighed heavily, and entered the house.

The woman and I sat drinking coffee and chatting aimlessly. She stuck a Marlboro in her mouth and I lit it with a Zippo. "I've seen you around," I told her, "Do you live here?"

"Yeah. I'm one a the ol man's daughters."

"You're very lucky."

"I knows it."

"What's your name?" I asked and she paused for a long moment, rolling her head around on her shoulders. I wondered how many warrants she had outstanding and what they were for.

"They's calls me Little Horse."

"Sogwil-usti?"

"Hahaha. That's close. That's good."

I lit a cigarette of my own and we smoked.

"You gotta woman, chooch?" She asked me.

"No," I said shaking my head.

"I ain't got no man neither. I jus kicked my last old man to de curb."

"Yeah?" I wondered if she meant that literally.

"Yeah, sometime it happens dat way innit?"

"Yeah. Sure enough."

"I ain't got no job neither," she said, "I needs to get a job."

"Yeah, well, maybe one will turn up."

"Well I won't get no job at tha Nation. They drug test and I like smokin that lef-hand bacca."

"Well, maybe you can get a job somewhere else."

"Mebbe so."

She told me a family of foxes had taken up residence that spring underneath a Cadillac parked out back. For some reason, the dogs had left them alone and the "mama fox" had whelped the youngsters right there, before moving deeper into the woods. We talked for a while and she re-filled our coffee cups and finally Dave came out of the house looking flushed and drained. We said our goodbyes and went and got in my truck and drove towards town. "I got the counter-smoke," Dave told me, "It's gonna go back twice as hard at whoever put it on me."

"I wouldn't want to be them," I said.

"Fuckin-A-Dude," We'll read in the paper bout what indian artist wraps his car around a tree in the next few weeks."

"The old man thought there was shit on you huh?"

"Yeah. He 'read on it.' Said sure enough. Gave me the counter-smoke and directions."

"Good deal, Dave."

"Hey man that was a little hottie you were hanging with there."

"Oh yeah. I think she was kinda flirting with me."

"Go for it dude. She's like totally fuckable."

"Dave, you think I want to hook-up with the medicine man's daughter?"

"Why not? You could be bullet-proof!"

"And what happens when I piss her off? I wake up and I been turned into a possum?"

"Always the realist," Dave shook his head.

"I can't help it."

A Short History

James Foreman killed Major Ridge and Stand Watie killed James Foreman and Anderson Springston was killed by a white man and Moses Alberty killed George Long and Jacob West killed Isaac Bushyhead and Tom Starr killed Benjamin Vore and Granville Rogers was killed by Braxton Nicholson and Charles Smith was killed by John Brown and John Smith was killed by Sheriff Boone and Stands Leaning was killed by Wheeler Fought and Wheeler Fought was hung by the Nation and Broom Baldridge was killed by Jim Starr and Tom Starr killed Ta-ka-to-ka and U.S. Deputy Smith killed Bean Starr and Tom Starr killed a negro and George Fields was killed by Martin Benge and John Ridge killed Judge Kell and Randolph Rogers killed a negro and unknown persons killed Bluford Rider and Charles Tikaneesky killed Moses Vickory and Richard Blackburn killed Columbus Vickory and David Nightkiller killed Elis Benge and Charles Webber killed Chunestootie and Dick Fields killed Andy Nave and Serge Beck was killed by Charley Rootdigger and Bud Trainor killed U.S. Deputy Dan Maples and Wes Bowman killed Ned Christie and Sam Sixkiller killed Dick Glass and Bill Goldsby killed Sequoyah Houston and U.S. Marshal Heck Thomas killed Texas Jack and Bill Goldsby killed Dick Richards and Henry Starr killed U.S. Deputy Floyd Wilson and Bill Goldsby was hung in Fort Smith and Tom Root killed U.S. Deputy Newton Leflore and Emmanuel Patterson killed Willard Ayers and Ezekial Proctor killed Lucy Beck and Sut Beck killed Johnson Proctor and Ezekial Proctor killed Sut Beck and U.S. Deputy Jim Owens killed William Hicks and George Hicks killed U.S. Marshal Jim Owens and Sam Sixkiller killed Jeter Thompson and U.S. Deputy Bass Reeves killed Bob Dozier and Jim Webb killed Reverend Steward and U.S. Deputy Bass Reeves killed Jim Webb and Frank Pierce killed Chub Moore and Grant Johnson killed Frank Wilson.

CARLOS' TALE

My old man had a mean streak and that's the truth. When he took a dog for a walk, he came back by himself, if you know what I mean. Mom said he got it in the war— operating that Browning on Tarawa and losing the hearing in his left ear made him mean. I don't know about that. I think he probably always had it. Well, hell, he spent the dirty thirties rustling cattle off cleared mesas in the Kiamichis and pulling hold-ups on both sides of the Red River. What does that tell you?

Somehow he ended up in Spain fighting with the Republicans in 1936 but all he would ever say about that was he spent every dime he had made as a mercenary for passage on one of the last ships out. Back in the states, he joined the army and went to farrier school and learned to make horseshoes out of bar stock and barbed wire and to shoe horses in the dark by touch and feel alone.

After the Japs bombed Pearl Harbor, the army decided it didn't farriers nearly as bad as it needed men with combat experience, so they made him a machinegun sergeant and sent him to the Pacific. He never said much about it, just told us some of the funny things like when a wop corporal won everybody's money at a card game one night and then got his head taken off by a Jap sniper first thing the next morning. Dad said bullets were flying in all directions and he ran out and got the money out of the dead wop's pockets. He said one of the privates said, "Sergeant McCoy, you're a bad man!" Dad thought that was funny as hell. He said he just told the kid, "He won't need the money where he's goin. Now shut up and shoot back at the sonsabitches!"

I believe that story. Dad always liked that money. And I remember him saying once when they were in the Philippines and setting up the Browning and a Jap came charging up on em and Dad shot him with his .45 and the Jap hit the ground. Dad said he just laid there dying and that I wouldn't believe the size of the worm that crawled out of his mouth. He told me that story to tell me why I shouldn't go barefoot around the hog pen.

Dad was forty-three years old when he came back in 1946, and when he married Mom, she was nineteen. That's how they did it back then. They bought a piece of woods outside of Wilburton and built em a shack and went to work with hogs and cattle and Dad shod horses all over the county. And that's how I grew up right there. Three sisters and me; I was the baby. We ate deer-meat and hog and ate poke weed and vegetables out of the garden. Dad loved to grow corn better than anything in the world and I remember he told me mule shit was better than horse shit on corn. I don't know, I never tried to grow any.

And the old man was a crack shot up until the day he died. I never saw him miss a target. I remember when I wanted to shoot the .45 he brought back from the army and he showed me how it worked and I couldn't hit the broad side of barn with it. Then he took it and aimed with one hand and hit the center of the target every time. Just *blam blam blam blam.* I asked him that day what it was like to shoot somebody and he said it was like shooting anything else—you just used the sights and squeezed the trigger.

He was out shoeing horses in the summer of 1970 and he ran off the road and crashed his truck and died. They think he might've had a heart attack that caused him to wreck. I don't know. I wish I'd talked to him more about all the things he knew, like shoeing horses and what he did in the war and all that. But I was just a kid. I thought he would be around forever.

HELL ON HORSES AND WOMEN

Mister McNair bought a quarter section in the Ouachita foothills from a full-blood Choctaw named Hand. Hand couldn't make any money farming without draft mules and the banks wouldn't loan him any money and he couldn't afford mama cows to start a beef herd. He had no money and no credit and no prospects for gaining either. So he sold the place to McNair and went fishing. That was 1910.

Mister and Mrs. McNair came up from northeast Texas with their two young daughters, all of them bumping and jolting in a covered wagon behind a four-mule team. Tied behind the wagon were a pair of cow ponies. They auctioned off almost everything they owned in Texas to afford this adventure. They bought the wagon and animals, tents, a cook stove, lanterns, and fencing tools and a Winchester rifle and Colt handgun. Mr. McNair was going into the cattle business.

Hand's old cabin was really just a tar paper shack; they used it as a kitchen and smokehouse. For the first three years they lived in tents, while McNair built a barn and corrals. The tents wore threadbare and drippy, but the house wasn't even begun until the barn was finished and when it was, the mules refused to enter. They thought the winter of '11 was the worst, freezing rain day after day followed by a foot of snow. Then the temperature didn't rise above freezing for sixteen days. They revised their expectations of how bad it could be after the summer of '12, thirty-five one-hundred degree days in a row and not a drop of rain the whole month of August. Their free-ranging cattle stayed scrawny but survived the weather and reproduced with regularity. The house was almost finished in the spring of 1913. McNair was fitting the store-bought windows in the rough frames when he heard their youngest daughter screaming in the woodline where she enjoyed looking for hen's eggs. A rattlesnake had bitten her. They buried her in the nearest cemetery.

Everything hurt Mrs. McNair worse after that; the cold winds blew right through her heart and the summer sun burnt her through her clothes. Before her daughter's death, she could accept the conditions: the bugs, the dirt, the filth. But after her little girl was gone, she found it all loathsome and daily tasks too monumental to perform. It was clear to her husband that she blamed him for their daughter's death. If they had stayed in Texas, the girl would still be alive, she thought. As grieved as he was, Mr. McNair thought better—there were rattlers in Texas, too. When the Lord calls you home you follow him, regardless of your age or place of residence, or so he thought to himself when the day's work was done and he could hand-roll some tobacco and drink a choc beer in the barn. His wife did not approve of these substances, alcohol and tobacco, but since moving to Oklahoma McNair had grown fond of each.

Later that year, Mrs. McNair caught the summer flu and it seemed she didn't have the strength to fight. The doctor came in his buggy but it made no difference. Mr. McNair buried her next to his daughter. That night, smoking in the barn, he sobbed and leaned against the wall. In a way, I killed them both, he thought, but that was fleeting madness and he knew it wasn't true. I've got to go on, he told himself, my little girl needs me and so do the mules and horses and cattle.

Three years passed with toil and heartache every day. McNair was proud of his daughter: she was tough as harness leather, absolutely unshakeable. This is what he told his new lady-friend whose name was Gretchen. She was almost half his age, the daughter of a retired U.S. Marshal named Hayes. Gretchen's mother was half-Choctaw and her dark eyes revived a flutter in McNair's heart that had been absent for years. The old Marshal approved of his daughter's suitor. McNair was no idler horse-thief drunkard. He was a hard-working fellow with the ambition to raise and sell good livestock. Just the type of man the new state needed. The two men discussed populist politics over tobacco while Gretchen and her mother fried chickens and mashed potatoes and McNair's daughter got licked all over by the Marshal's hounds.

McNair and Gretchen married in May, 1917. As a wedding gift, the old Marshal bought the newlyweds the half-section adjoining McNair's property. Eleven months later, they had a new baby boy, Hayes McNair, and six-hundred and forty acres to fence. The cattle herd increased every year.

Gretchen had been born and reared in the defunct Choctaw Nation and she could work like a grown man in trousers when she wasn't laid up with the sickness or pregnant. She mortified the Texas cowboys McNair hired as day-labor by squatting by the branding fire and fishing fresh-severed calf testicles out of the flame with a Bowie knife. She would just laugh and blow on the testicles to cool them before chomping them up and swallowing.

Southeast Oklahoma had worn off on McNair as well: the house was never finished, the plans abandoned in the quest to clear more land and then fence it and then buy still more. The dirt floor remained for a decade. When the family, now with three sons and McNair's daughter, completely outgrew the hovel, McNair hired Italian carpenters from Krebs to build a decent house while he worked with the cows.

By the time Wall Street fell, the boys were old enough to build fence on their own. The bottom fell out of the cattle market, too. McNair had seen it coming and he knew it would not come back in a month or even a year. He wrangled up a job as a mail carrier, delivering the mail on a mule and maintaining one of the few paying jobs in the county. His neighbors scoffed at the sight of a rancher delivering the mail, but one by one they went broke and McNair bought their places for pennies on the dollar. Gretchen kept chickens and raising piglets to slaughter; she fed them kitchen scraps and homegrown corn.

When the big war brought beef prices back, McNair owned twenty-eight hundred acres and the boys were still clearing brush and building fence.

When McNair was more than sixty years of age, the army took his oldest boy, Hayes. The old man quit his mail delivery route and went back to the cows full-time. His wife took a tumble off a cow pony and was banged up bad. She started staying close to the house more and more, finding religion to pray for her son in the war.

While Hayes packed mules for Merrill in Burma, McNair read week-old newspapers from Oklahoma City and watched the war progress. The President had declared cattle-raising an "industry of critical importance," thus sparing his two youngest sons from the draft. They built up the ranch to its full carrying capacity, working six days a week year after year. When the war was finally over, Hayes McNair came home with only one slight bullet wound and his two younger brothers went off to college. They had had enough of the cow shit and dust and backbreaking labor.

Hayes, however, had the itch. He could not believe how his father had aged; now he was an old man. His mother, too, had shrunk in stature and seemed permanently saddened. He agreed with his father on only two subjects—the importance of always voting Democratic and that a man could make a helluva lot of money out here raising cattle. If only he could manage the grass and keep the brush and saplings beat back that charged against the improved pasture every spring. Hayes wanted to do it—it was tough living but gravy compared to Burma. He smoked and thought of a dozen ways he could improve the ranch.

"After I'm dead do whatever you want. Just take care of your Mama," McNair told his son, "But until then I'm the boss."

"Sure Pa." Hayes went along with direction but he made one thing clear—he was only working five days a week. Unlike his father, he had interests outside of the bovine. Hell, he was twenty-five years old. He needed to find a wife.

He found her working in a drugstore in Antlers. She was just a kid, but beautiful, a redhead ready to flee her hard-shell Baptist preacher-man father. He tipped his cowboy hat and said, "Yes Ma'am," and they fell in love right there by the soda fountain. When they married, she was pregnant and his father was dying from the lungs out. They named the baby boy Joseph, after Hayes's father who had just gone to rest in the cemetery. Little Joe was a happy baby, all giggles and grins but Maggie soon learned what she was in for. The ranch was a long, dusty, bumping ride outside of town. Hayes started to drink and when he drank he smashed things and brandished guns and cursed imaginary Japanese. Soon she was pregnant again and the summer was blistering, their house like an oven. The baby was a girl and Hayes had no interest in her.

One day, Maggie had a Jack Daniels and Coca-Cola and the edge came off. She started drinking them every day. The two of them kept the bootlegger in business for a few years until one day a Hereford bull pinned Hayes up against a gate and broke him up real bad. The doctor said he was lucky to make it to the hospital. Weeks later the same doctor said he was lucky to be wheeled out. Hayes swore he would never work stock drunk again. Since he worked stock every day, he never picked up another bottle. Maggie kept at it, though, and it sickened Hayes. He'd come home tired, leaning on his cane, and he could smell her roasting in the bourbon. They held it together with pretense for another decade and then divorced. She took the daughter with her and Hayes wrote Maggie a check for ten-thousand dollars. He never spoke to her again.

Joe graduated from high school in 1964 and he would have been a top hand in any outfit. He knew broncs and green colts and workhorses. He could pull breach calves and castrate young bulls and repair trucks and tractors and downed fence. Hayes wanted him to go to ag school in Stillwater but Joe wanted to rodeo. "That's a fool idea," his Dad told him, "I'm so crippled up I can hardly get around. What happens if you git neck-broke? Who the hell is gonna run this place?"

"Hell, I ain't gonna get hurt."

"Anybody can git hurt."

"Well I ain't gonna."

Joe could hardly believe it; his Dad's eyes were tearing up. I guess he really loves me, Joe thought, and then he hit the rodeo circuit. For two years he rode saddle broncs from Alberta to west Texas. He never got hurt, at least not real bad, but he never did make a lot of money either. What he did was fall in love with the wildest little barrel-racing gal he had ever laid eyes on. She had long blonde hair and just about the most jumping-out paint horse he could imagine. That horse could flat-out move, and Becky rode him like the champion her collection of belt buckles proved her to be. Becky was from western Oklahoma, which is almost like a separate country from Joe's native eastern hill country, but east met west and wild passion ensued.

They did bourbon shots in rodeo grounds parking lots and then they'd rut like whitetail deer in October. They got married in Hot Springs on Joe's twenty-first birthday and showed up trailing dust on the long ranch road that led to Hayes' front porch. Hayes knew something was up when he saw his son's truck pull up with a blonde in the passenger seat and a new trailer attached to the hitch. Inside the trailer was a paint horse. "That ain't like Joe," his father said to himself, "To own a paint. Surely he's got more sense than that." Joe got out of the truck all smiles like when he was two years old.

"Dad," he said, "I got married."

"Well hells bells," Hayes shifted his cane to his left hand and held out his right to welcome his new daughter-in-law. "Welcome to the family," he said.

"I'm just happy to be here," Becky was giggling and flushed, "You have a beautiful ranch."

"It's just what it is." Hayes turned to his son, "I bought George Landry's big pasture last week."

"Really?"

"Yeah. Seven-hundred and twenty acres. Jus needs to be fenced."

They all laughed like old friends.

The baby came a year later; they named him David after Becky's father. Joe hung up his fancy rodeo spurs and settled down to ranching. They had always used cow horses to cut out calves on the ranch but they were just grade horses without any registration. Even when he was young, Joe could train a horse to do anything and he entered his horses in quarter horse competitions and won. Now, what he really wanted to do with the ranch was breed the best quarter horses in the country. Once he made up his mind to breed horses, Joe started going to the big horse sales in Texas and buying high-dollar brood mares. He bred them to studs out of the ranch's working stock. The result was some fine horseflesh. The colts were born with cow sense, the desire and ability to work a herd of cows with minimal input from the human riding atop. They could move with lightning speed in any direction and slide to a stop out of a gallop in their own body length. It required an expert rider to even stay mounted on one of these horses but Joe could do it—he understood a horse from the sole of its hoof to the twitch of its ears.

By 1980, he was breeding the best quarter horses in Oklahoma. Some of the old-timers said they were probably the best cow ponies ever foaled in the state. Joe would just smile and nod. He knew they were damn fine horses. Somewhere along the line, between horse sales in Lubbock and cutting horse shows in Wichita, he and Becky drifted apart. She took Dave and the girls and moved back to her father's ranch. When she asked Joe for a divorce, it threw him for a loop, but he rolled back to his feet just like he did in his old rodeo days. Within a year he had married again, to a gal from Antlers, but she couldn't take the isolation of living on a ranch where the nearest beer and cigarettes were a thirty-mile drive away. She left him for an insurance salesman.

Joe wasn't surprised to see her go. He knew it was a mistake to have married her to begin with. Besides, he had other priorities. He had the best green horse coming along that he had ever seen. Of course, the horse could move, all of Joe's horses could move. But this little fella seemed to be able to read Joe's mind. He barely needed cues—he wanted a human on his back and he wanted to cut cows with every fiber in his one-thousand pounds. Joe knew he was a one-in-a-million-horse. He had the moves and the confirmation and the heart and the temperament and the concentration. Joe named him Lucky Strike.

Joe let Lucky Strike mature so he wouldn't blow his joints. Then he started winning money on him. He had the best cutting horse in the country and he knew it and for the first time in a decade he let himself relax. Everything that flowed out of him seemed to be flowing back. Becky began calling him on the phone and they reconciled and remarried and she brought the kids back to live on the ranch. Lucky Strike was like a big pet for all of them. He lived in the back yard and when they woke up in the mornings, he was looking in the windows and whinnying for grain.

Lucky Strike and Joe won the state cutting horse championships in Oklahoma, Kansas and Missouri. There was an article on the horse and rider in *Cutting Horse Journal* and the pair appeared on the cover of *Western Horseman* magazine. In 1987, they won the World Championship in Fort Worth and Joe was handed a prize check for one-hundred-thousand dollars. The next morning they were loading up for the drive home and a big hatted Texan with a gold Rolex showed Joe a check with his name on it. The check was made out for one-hundred seventy-five thousand dollars. The Texan wanted to buy Lucky Strike. Joe just laughed at him.

Memorial Day, 1988: the whole family was gathered in Joe and Becky's backyard grilling up steaks and laughing up a storm. Dave wanted to go riding so he saddled up a green horse while his Dad saddled up Lucky Strike. They rode off like cowboys hitting cowtown while Becky finished her ninth beer of the day. Joe and Dave rode all over the ranch, talking about the old days and what needed to be done to improve carrying capacity. Darkness began to fall as they were riding down the big timbered hill the family called "the mountain." For no reason, Lucky Strike stumbled with a gut-wrenching snap and went down in a heap. Joe leapt free of the wreck but just barely, and when he got to his feet, he knew it was over. He fought like a Brangus bull to hold the tears back, but he couldn't do it. Lucky Strike was leg-broke. Dave was pale and wide-eyed. "Go back to my truck and get the .357 out of the glove box," Joe told him and the boy was gone, throwing gravel and quirting his horse.

Becky, Dave and old Hayes took the truck back out to the downed horse and found Joe there lying on Lucky Strike's head to keep him calm and on the ground. Hayes hobbled over and handed his son the .357 revolver. "Sorry son," was all he could choke out and Joe nodded, trying not vomit, then stepped back and shot the horse between the eyes.

Joe lost his interest in horses. He kept a few around because Dave enjoyed them and wanted to learn the business. But Joe washed his hands of cutting horse stock. He got into registered Angus cattle and bought a pair of saddle mules out of southwest Missouri to use as his personal mounts.

Dawn at the ranch. Dave eased to his feet like a man twice his age and stuck a Marlboro in his mouth. Rachel was already up with the T.V. on, a baby on her hip, and a toddler tugging on her sweatpants. "Is the coffee on?" He asked and struck the last match out of the pack.

"Dammit Dave," her voice broke like glass, "Is that all you can say? 'Is the coffee on? Is breakfast ready?'"

"I'll skip the eggs but I would like some coffee."

"Am I not getting through to you? I'm sick of all this." She started crying while Dave was pulling on his boots. His hands were full of rope burns and rasp scratches and it hurt to bend his fingers.

"Are you ever gonna talk to me?" Rachel sobbed, "Why can't you act like a human?"

"Dad went to Wyoming to buy herd bulls."

"What does that have to do with anything?"

"It means I don't have time for this shit. I've got a hundred and thirty cows to feed and eleven colts to green break."

"I hate you. I hate living like this."

Dave left the trailer and drove thirty miles to the convenience store and bought two cups of coffee and a breakfast burrito. Then he drove thirty miles back to the ranch to feed the cattle. He was backing the dually out of the barn when he heard both back tires on one side hissing. He got out of the truck cursing a blue streak and got down on his knees to inspect the deflating tires. He had found the two bolts off the tractor that had been lost months before. Jesus Christ, he thought, what's the chance of that? His Dad had the tire-repair kit and was presently driving north.

Dave pulled the listing dually out of the way, and, taking a cup of coffee, he got back in his little Nissan truck. He backed the Nissan into to the barn and began loading bales of alfalfa onto it. Dave loaded bales until the little truck was overflowing. Then, he threw bales on top of the cab and some bales onto the hood. With the Nissan sagging under the load and Dave barely able to see over the bales on the hood, he crept in low gear down the ranch road. He had to look out the window to navigate. He sipped the now-cool coffee and lit a cigarette. As he passed the trailer, Rachel flung open the front door and screamed at him. "I hate you!" she shrieked and Dave just nodded and gave a slight wave. "You're an asshole!" She continued a litany of verbal abuse and he turned up the weather forecast.

He drove on past the trailer and out into the east section where the one-hundred-and-thirty mama cows were expecting spring calves and awaiting green grass. They were usually fed out of the white Ford dually and at first they just stared at the grey Nissan, but when Dave jumped out and dumped alfalfa, the cows mooed loudly and started for the truck at a trot. Dave drove forward about fifty feet, dumped a few bales, then drove another fifty feet and repeated the process. He made a big half-circle and with all the alfalfa expended, he headed back to the barn. He got up into third gear on the ranch road, hitting forty miles per hour as he passed the trailer, giving Rachel no further chance to harangue him. He backed into the barn, re-loaded the Nissan to sagging, and headed again to the east section to finish feeding.

As he made his second trip, creeping past the trailer in the overloaded Nissan, Rachel rushed out on the plywood porch, this time with his Marlin .45-70 rifle in her hands. *Ka-Boom!* She fired it into the air and worked the lever and fired again—*Ka-Boom!* "You're going to listen to me fucker!" She screamed, "You can't ignore me!" Dave did not slow down and he did not increase speed. He just shook his head. *Goddamn, I always did like a hot-blooded little brood mare.*

On the second trip, the mama cows greeted the grey Nissan with enthusiasm. Dave finished feeding them then made a drive around the section's fence line to make sure everything was in good order. The big wind the night before had dropped limbs onto the fence and Dave pulled them out of the wire one by one. Out by Lucky Strike's grave. Dave got out of the truck and leaned against the hood. He checked his watch—it read 10:40. He dug around in the Nissan's ashtray until he found a half-smoked joint and he leaned against the truck and smoked on it until the tiny cherry of flame burnt his fingers. Then he smoked a Marlboro and drank the rest of his cold coffee while staring into the brushy side of the fence. His mind wandered through cutting horse genealogies and varmint rifle ballistic coefficients. Well hells bells, he thought, I'd better run back to the store and get a tire repair kit. The Nissan's spare was shredded and he figured he would be truly fucked if he got another flat.

Stranded, with a bunch of pregnant registered Angus cows and a crazy woman who had a key to his gun safe. He couldn't let that happen.

He left the ranch via the back way, avoiding the trailer and bumping along primitive gravel roads until he pulled out on pavement and drove the thirty miles back to the store. They were sold out of tire-repair kits so he drove another ten miles into Antlers where he bought a decent kit at the automotive store. Then he had a double cheese coney and fries and an XL iced tea at the Sonic Drive-In. Then he drove forty miles back to the ranch, stopping at the store for a six-pack of beer.

Dave parked the little truck next to the big one and went to work fixing the flats. With this accomplished, he wheeled the air-compressor out of the barn and started inflating the first tire. The colts, curious about the commotion, came up and watched him intently, their heads hanging over the fence. He took the opportunity to slip halters on the calmest four, and one by one he lead them over to the circular horse-walker where he snapped their leads onto the rotating machine's lumbering arms. When the four colts were attached, he turned the machine on and the horses began walking in a circle, following the arms tugging them forward. "That'll get your ya-yas out," he told the circulating horses and he went back to the barn to switch the air-compressor over to the other tire.

When both tires were inflated and the colts had marched for an hour, he stopped the machine. He took the horses one at a time into the fifty-foot round pen and hooked them up to a long line. Then, with the line in one hand and a whip in the other, he worked them at a walk, trot, and canter around the pen, whoaing and giddying them with light touches of the whip. The horses are performing well, he thought, they're a good buncha colts. When they had all learned their lessons to his satisfaction, he lead them back to the pasture, two colts lead with each hand.

I got an hour of sunlight left, maybe an hour and a half, Dave thought. He walked over to the dually and fetched the bolt-action .243 and a pair of binoculars out from behind the seat. He hung them from the gun rack in the Nissan and drove over and through brush, then parked on a slight hill overlooking the grazing mama cows. He pulled a ratty and rotting camp chair out of the Nissan's bed and sat with the sun descending behind him, glassing the grass and brush clumps for a pack of coyotes assembling to rampage. He rolled a joint and smoked it. He lit a Marlboro as the sun fell to its cradle and no coyotes appeared.

Dave drove home to the trailer expecting the worst but his expectations were unfulfilled. The kids were happy to see him and he teased them and laughed at his own jokes. Rachel eyed him with stoicism. "I'm making burgers. Do you wanna piece of bacon on one?"

"Sure hon, thanks."

Dave stuck the six-pack in the fridge and grabbed a warm one to drink. After dinner, the kids went to sleep and Rachel came in and sat on the couch where Dave was watching CNN. She fished one of his cigarettes out of the hard pack. "Why did your dad go to Wyoming to buy bulls?" she asked.

"They got the best Angus money can buy."

Rachel nodded, "You know your dad's been married three times?"

"Yeah, but he married my mom twice."

"She left him both times."

"My mom's a drunk."

"I understand why now." She eyed him and realized he did not understand anything. She watched as he pulled a tick off his ankle and smashed it against the coffee table with a Bic lighter.

"I don't know if I want my kids to grow up out here," she said, "There aren't many outlets."

"Hon, there ain't no forty-two-hundred acre cattle ranches close to town."

"I'm sure that's true."

"Hell, I grew up here. Mostly."

"I know. But you are a crazy person."

"Shit. I'm just tryin to make a living."

"I want my son to know how to be in a relationship."

Dave just shrugged. He doesn't understand anything that's not covered in fur, she thought. She went to check on the children and saw they were sleeping. She watched them slumber for a long time. When she went back to the living room, Dave was slumped over, snoring on the couch. She started to cry but then went to their bedroom and packed her clothes.

FRAGMENT

The Johnson boys were Arkansas hill trash, Jonah being half-smart and Daniel being half-crazy. They were both too lazy to take part in Mr. Lincoln's army or the CSA. Running with the guerrillas was hard work, too, with nary a piece of pie after dinner. The Draft Laws convinced them to go on the scout in the Cherokee Nation. They only got to steal a few horses before losing their hearts to a pair of pretty full-blood girls, the Fivekiller sisters. Those girls were sweet on those redheaded Arkies as well and the boys traded the stolen Creek horses to the Fivekiller clan and married the girls, thinking they'd prosper as farmers and maybe get rich selling corn liquor to their heathen in-laws. But the war raged on year after year, Jayhawkers stole all their beeves, and Quantrill's men shot all their hogs. The boys and their wives (both now pregnant) set up a make-shift camp high in the Cookson Hills and spent their time hiding out from everyone.

After the war, it was almost worse. There was not enough money to buy nor sell and only starvation was free. There were not hardly enough good horses left to steal. After stumbling for years through these challenges the Johnson boys found neither prosperity nor salvation. All they found was more mixed-blood babies crawling on the rocky dirt floor of sawmill plank cabins.

The brothers finally made a batch of liquor that was sale-able and they cashed out, hearing there was big money in buffalo hides if a crew could bring them back in off the prairie. They bought a good pair of mules out of Carthage Missouri, a wagon, and outfits to match. They special-ordered a pair of Sharp's .50-.90 rifles and had one of them fitted with a telescopic sight. They planned to use their wives as skinners and their brother-in-law Hindfoot came along with his wife as well. With hides selling for $3.50 each, a fortune seemed assured. The brothers left their children with their in-laws and the three couples moved out west, the wagon creaking and the mules sweating.

They never came back from the plains. "Comanche," the old folks said.

THARP'S TALE

I went poachin one time. Knew it wasn't right but I did it anyway. I went an cast offa county road with a sorry no good for nuthin hog hunter wannabe an I came damn close to getting killed an then goin to jail cause of it.

There wuz three of us. It was me and Turd Head#1 and Turd Head#2. We all brought our best bay dogs as well as a good catch dog. #2 was too much of a sissy-boy to bring a catch dog so he jus brung a pup I gave him. My good lookin gyp got hoggy in the box so we cast her and a dog named Rebel and #1's pride and joy pot-lickin cur. They hit a hard track and I knew from watchin my gyp leave that she wuz gonna bay up right quick so I opened up the dog box and turned #2's pup loose behind them. She dilly-dallied around some and I hissed her an she soon left out. We had a pow-wow real quick waitin for the dogs to hit an since we wuz poachin on a county road we decided two of us should go to the dogs an one should stay behind with the catch dog and the truck. Well for some reason I had no gun that night but #1 had a .357 pistol under the front seat of the truck.

We decided that me and #2 would head to the dogs on foot and that #2 would pack the heat. This wuz Sans Bois country, lots of Russian hogs and just plain tough country, steep cliffs, ravines, and dry creeks with lots of ankle-bustin rocks. The dogs lit up in the hills about that time and I could hear them splitting into two bays. Our three main dogs were in a ravine bayed up and my friend's pup was a little ways off by herself bayed up. I took off like a bolt of fat boy lightning towards my old gyp an the better soundin bay. I wuz thinking #2 wuz right behind me with the gun. For whatever reason I doan know, my houla went to my buddy's pup and #1's pit gyp went to his other dog as well as #2's gyp. I heard my houla hit that pig that the pup had been baying and from the squeal I could tell it wuz jus a little shoat. They wuz a good ways off an I reckoned they would have that shoat dead before I could get to em.

Meanwhile, the pit an the rest of the dogs was fightin a young boar in a hole. An soon as I git there #1's junk pit turned that boar loose on me. The sucker wuz maybe two hunnert and fifty pounds of Russian boar an lucky for my behind the houlas got that hog down right at my feet an I stabbed him and cut his throat. So I start lookin for #2 who is supposed to be backing me up with the gun. Of course he's a dip shit an no where to be found. I wuz mad as hell. The houlas are still clamped on this big dead Russian boar an I pry em off an tie em to trees an start walkin back to the truck to get #1 to help haul that boar back to the road. I come outta the woods an see a Sheriff's Deputy pulled over behind the truck. Fuck me, I sez, we may be goin to jail for this hunt but #1 was givin the deputy a great bullshit story bout how we started out on land we had permission to hunt but the dogs bayed elsewhere. The deputy believed all this an went on his way and I said—where the holy hell is #2? An then we found out he wuz hidin in the woods since he wuz packin a piece an had warrants outta Texas. He kinda lost his cool when he seen that deputy. So we went back an got the boar an the dogs an I reckoned to hell with huntin with those two turd heads again. #1's dogs were shit but he could talk the bark offa tree.

PASTOR JOHN'S TALE

They bin tryin to get me to join the Identity movement for seventeen years. I like em, they're good people, but theys crazy and it's unscriptural. You see I grew up down there in southeast Arky-saw livin wit the coloreds. We caught catfish outta the same mud hole if you know what I mean. We lived in that county cheek by jowl, and no Identity preacher can tell me the colored man is the beast of the field. Anybody ever see a Hereford bull that can quote scripture? Huh? Or a brush-eatin goat that knows the steps to eternal salvation? It's crazy. I know Bible-believing coloreds that can outpreach any Identity man ol Pastor Peters included. They can quote scripture frontwards and backwards all day long standin on theys head. So don't be telling me the colored ain't a man with an eternal soul cause I know better. I mean I like Identity people and they like my preachin but theys crazy and it's unscriptural.

And it's all Jew this and Jew that. Son, there ain't a damn Jew in eighty miles of here so what's the problem?

I ain't got to truck with the international banker, the money-lendin one-worlder, that is true. No honest man has truck wit a money-lendin parasite be that banker blood-sucker Jew or Gentile. Jesus ran the moneylenders out of the temple. He was not panty-waist sissy. He was a man's man. If Jesus were alive today he would own a semi-automatic high-powered rifle! See that's what Identity people like about my preachin. I tell it like it is. I ain't one of these beat around the bush Babtist horn blowers. But they don't like it when I tell them their hellish perverted doctrine is unscriptural and they should love the colored like they love themselves.

It ain't the international money-lendin Jew that's the white man's problem. It ain't the Jew puttin the beer in the workingman's hand, it ain't the Jew puttin the cigarette in his mouth. Same wit the colored, ain't no big banker puttin' the crack in his pipe. The problem with the white man is the white man. Problem wit the colored is the colored. And they both got the same problem—they don't know Jesus! They love that fishin boat and beer can more than they love their Savior who hung on a cross to wash away their sins!

I bin there. I know. I bin a guttersnipe drunk. I bin a degenerate hop-headed fool. I took every drug you can imagine. I took em all at the same time. The booze, the pot, the acid, the speed, I took em all. I'd git so turned around and outta my head I wouldn't know where I was at or where I had bin. Couldn't even tell if I was layin in a cornfield or walking down the street. I was a turned around mixed up mashed potato head. One night I took all them drugs as many as I could find. I was drinkin, smoking, snortin, swallowin. Went with my so-called friends to the big Hank Williams Junior and David Allen Coe show in Tulsa. How we ever got here I don't know.

We wuz a confused bunch of fools. And by the grace of Almighty God we made it back home alive without getting killed or killin someone else.

That night I wuz layin in my bed with all that poison in my head. The walls of that trailer wuz waving and flowin in my eyes. The bed was spinnin and I had to grab aholdt of the bed posts to keep from being thrown into the deep. It went on like that for hours. Then I heard two voices as loud as thunder inside my head. It was Jesus and the Devil discussin who would have my soul. "He's no good to you," the Devil said, "Let me have him for my demonic kingdom of Hell." "No," says Jesus, "There might be hope for this wretched fool yet." The Devil kept talkin, tryin to talk Jesus into givin up on me. I jus started weeping like a baby. I jumped outta bed and fell on my knees before Almighty God. I got to beggin and pleadin the Lord Jesus Christ not to let the Devil have me for his Satanic Hell. When you call upon the Lord the Devil must depart and that's what happened. I took refuge in the Rock of Almighty God!

Since that night I ain't takin a drinky-drink, a smokey-smoke, or a sniffy-sniff. I decided I wanted to be a pastor. I wanted to increase and uplift the flock. I went to Bible college in Oklahoma City. I got there and they wanted me to learn Greek. 'Greek,' I says, 'I cain't hardly speak English. I don't wanna do no pastorin in Greece!' 'No,' they says, 'It's to help you study the Bible in the original.' So I learned their Greek and took their classes. I learnt, though, that most of the men there weren't called by God to pastor. They jus wanted a job where they could make a livin without doin any work. There wuz one fella there from Alabama and we became good friends, brothers in Christ. He's the one who first told me about the New World Order. We did our own studying on the side, started asking questions of the teachers they weren't man enough to answer. For instance, what did Jesus tell the Pharisees? He looked em right in the eye and said, 'You are of your father—the Devil!' That's what Jesus thought about the so-called authorities of his day. I'd like to look some of the Senator big-shot muckety-mucks in the eye and tell em the same thing! If I ever see one I will! Well the Pharisees of the Bible College asked us to leave and we did.

I believe a pastor should work as his flock works so I came back here and took a job at the sawmill. By the grace of God I found a saintly woman to marry. I preached on Sundays for years and finally the Lord's people began to flock to hear my preachin. Old woman Turner signed over a barn to us and we painted it white and put up a cross and made that our church.

That's jus me, workin for the Lord and lovin every minute of life. This week I bought my daughter a dulcimer so she can play and sing those good ol gospel songs. Other than that, I jus bin reading the Bible and pastorin and birthin lambs. First two lambs wuz born dead an we jus pray the good Lord blesses us with triplets on the next ewe!

HOLLIS' TALE

Don't let anybody bullshit you. Unless you inherit it, there's only two ways to put together a big ranch. Hard work? No. Luck? No. Timing? Forget about it. Only two ways: marry into good grass and/or commit crime. I guess that's the way it's always been. This was once all indian land, ain't hardly none of it indian land now. And where did the indians get it? From other indians. It's all in the history books no one reads. The Cherokees stole it from the Osage and the white men stole it from the Cherokees. And then the rich man stole it from the poor man and the rich man intends to keep it."

Most of what you have around here I wouldn't even call ranches. More like hobby farms. These ol boys raise just enough cows to depress the price for everybody. They got forty, sixty, eighty acres. A thirty-thousand dollar truck with hydraulic round bale spears. Four-wheel-drive tractors. Rural water district water. A solid steady job in town. Lines of credit from the bank or credit union. Everything purchased and bought, everything handed to them. And all they can do with all they have is to take six months to make seventy-five dollars on a feeder steer. And how they love seein those cows come in! Something to do with their grandsons I guess. It's easy to raise cows if you got a pension comin in. Or at least it used to be. What with feed prices nowadays, it's an expensive hobby. I stole the term from somebody I don't remember who— it's romantic capitalism.

SMOKE

He had been raised real traditional backwoods Creek indian but he hadn't spoken a word of Mvskoke in years. And he didn't go see his relatives at the dances. He didn't give a shit. What he did was paint. And he was good at it. He had always painted and he had always been good. But now, after decades, the money was rolling in. He had art in galleries all over the United States. Some people wanted him to go to Germany. It was good times. He was almost fifty years old and finally he was making a good living with art. He had a Cadillac, jewelry, a couple of young girlfriends. He wanted to party. The years of working minimum wage shit jobs were over. He wanted to get wild. And he did.

If you've got the money you can find a party in Muskogee any night of the week. And he usually found one. It was a Thursday morning, 9:55 AM. He and some friends had snorted speed and drank all night and he was ready to keep going. He was so drunk he could barely walk so he got his friend, a Cherokee, to drive him in the

Cadillac to the liquor store. They were sitting in the parking lot waiting for the store to open and finally the clock struck 10. He gave his friend some money for a bottle of whiskey and a couple of six-packs of strong beer and waited in the Cadillac's passenger seat.

For no reason except boredom, he opened the car's glove box and took out his .44 magnum. He swung the cylinder open and there was only one bullet in it. Where the other five bullets went he had no idea. He thought the missing bullets were funny and he laughed. A black guy, a derelict was approaching the liquor store's front door and on impulse he called out to him, "Hey, nigger . . ." The man looked over at him and he pointed the .44 at the guy and pulled the trigger. Click. The hammer fell on an empty chamber. The black guy turned and ran and he laughed uproariously at the fellow's expense.

He could see his friend through the liquor store's window. He was at the counter paying and had missed the grand joke. Still laughing, without even thinking about it, he swung the revolver's cylinder open again. Still one bullet. He closed the gun. He liked the *click* it made. He held the gun to the side of his head and pulled the trigger. The hammer fell on the live round and blew his brains across the Cadillac's interior.

STATE TROOPER

Paul Johnson grew up in the southside suburbs of Tulsa, a white kid in a white town. His parents were staid, churchgoing Baptists who were ever eager not to offend and who avoided any adventures beyond the boundaries of the proper. Paul idolized his uncle who was an Oklahoma Highway Patrol trooper and got called away from family functions to work accident scenes on rain-slick highways. Paul's mother wanted him to be a teacher or work in a climate-controlled office and his father just slept on the couch after work. Paul rebelled against these expectations of mediocrity by wanting to be just like his uncle. He wanted to wear the Smokey the Bear hat and carry a handgun and be a state trooper. His uncle coached him through the process of his ambition, telling the teenager that he should never smoke marijuana and that he should get a college degree in criminal justice with a minor in Spanish. Paul jumped through these hoops and was accepted into the Oklahoma Highway Patrol

Academy and graduated with his mother crying throughout the ceremony.

The state sent new troopers where they were needed, while troopers with seniority usually requested and were given placements near their hometowns and families. Paul's uncle had warned him of this. He could forget all about being stationed near the urban centers of Oklahoma City or Tulsa. If he was lucky, his uncle told him, they'd assign him out west where there were not many people and not many problems. If he was unlucky he'd get a post in one of the hellholes of the eastern Oklahoma hill country. Paul considered himself unlucky when he found out he had been assigned to the Stilwell office in one of the eastern counties that bordered Arkansas. "It's the armpit of the state," his uncle told him, "Wear your Kevlar everywhere."

Paul had never been east of Tulsa, and armed with his uncle's advice and his new badge and guns, he drove to Stilwell to rent an apartment. He soon found out that there were no apartments to lease, at least not any that were not sagging, rodent-infested, and shell-shocked from years of abuse. A trailer was unacceptable to him, so he ended up leasing a paint-peeled, weather-burdened house that was one room wide and three rooms deep. The house was pitiful but Paul consoled himself that he was only here long enough to get enough seniority to get back to Tulsa.

They had given him a detailed topo map of the county but during his first day on patrol it became apparent that the map bore little resemblance to reality. None of the county roads were marked. It was often difficult to tell what was a county road and what was an extended driveway—the locals often lived in a cluster of houses and trailers that were a half-mile or more off the road. Roads that the map showed as existent were not and roads and gravel trails that were not shown on the map were everywhere, snaking without apparent reason into the forest. All the ditches were mulched with fast food wrappers, ripped up feed sacks, and beer cans. Cattle wandered aimlessly down the middle of back roads, stepping slowly over discarded articles of clothing and spent shotgun shells. Paul had never seen anything like it. Hell, he had never seen anything remotely like it. The locals sometimes had eight or ten junked or wrecked cars, trucks, and tractors lined up, rusting amidst weeds surrounding an unleveled doublewide trailer that sat within spitting distance of a dilapidated century-old farmhouse. Horses or cattle sometimes appeared hanging their heads out of the old houses' windows. Others had stacks of mosquito-harboring used tires as tall as a man and twenty feet long. A lifetime's worth of tires hoarded for no apparent reason. And then along the shoulders of SH82, entire yards were made up of junk lined in rows with signs reading, "Everthin For Sale."

His fellow troopers told him to always watch his back. "Don't follow anyone into the woods out here," they told him. "We got some bad boys. And don't underestimate the women. Last year a sixteen year-old girl, dead drunk, pulled a .44 magnum on me." "Hell yes," the oldest and wisest of his trooper comrades joined in, "We got everything out here—dope growers, meth-makers, moonshiners, crazy indians, neo-Nazis, outlaw bikers, you name it." Paul nodded. It was clear that he was much further from Tulsa than the maps indicated. It was almost like another country, he thought, like South America or something.

As every newly-hired law enforcement officer does, Paul fantasized endlessly about shooting someone. In grocery stores buying hamburger patties or parked outside drive-ins, he would run scenarios through his head of how he would survive close quarters combat. He never imagined being shot for no reason during a routine traffic stop or missing a turn at 90 mph. Those possibilities were too likely and mundane to consider.

Working the graveyard shift—eleven at night to seven in the morning—Paul put on his pressed uniform and shiny boots, the .357 Sig on his right hip and the air weight .38 snubnose holstered to his left ankle. He carried a folding knife clipped to his right front pocket and a German switchblade in the left one. Thus arrayed, he set out to write speeding tickets and pull over swerving drivers. A very high percentage of drivers in Adair County had either a headlight non-functional or tail or brake lights busted or burnt out. After the first few shifts Paul quit pulling people over for such minor infractions of state law. Mostly, he arrested drunk drivers. About half the time, when he searched the drunk's, vehicle he would find meth or marijuana. Working traffic accidents became routine. After the first few bad ones, he learned to depersonalize the blood and suffering. If children were involved it was tougher to take, but Paul learned to flip the internal switch and just do his job.

Sometime during his first year, Paul realized it was all just a game. The county jail in Stilwell was so small that unless someone committed murder or a violent crime they would not remain incarcerated for long. A simple shooting rarely resulted in a felony indictment. Oklahoma had retained its 19th century standards of what constituted a "legal shooting." Adair County had a number of residents who had been involved in numerous of gunfights and shootings. A few had histories that would have qualified them as gunfighters in the Old West. And the further east one went within the state, the more hesitant county D.A.'s were to issue a first degree murder indictment.

One early morning, having coffee and eggs with two of his fellow troopers, Paul was amazed to learn there had not been a felony drug conviction in the county court for over a decade. His jaw dropped.

"Amazing, ain't it?" His buddy, Jim "Smitty" Smith filled him in: "We bust em, they can't make bail and they sit in the jail until the Sheriff needs bunk space. Then they turn em loose. Usually months later, the charges are just dropped."

Paul shook his head, "Jesus," he muttered.

"That's the way it is," Smitty continued, "The feds have taken some boys out of here, and the OSBI once in a blue moon. But no local felony dope convictions. It just doesn't happen."

Smitty took a sip of his black coffee. "This is between us, Bro. Understand? The thing to do here is lay low. Just do your job. Let the bullshit roll off your back. It's been outlaw country here for a hundred-and-fifty years. We ain't gonna change it."

"That's right," said "Big Tom" Turner, the oldest and grayest of the troopers in the diner that morning. "And don't trust anyone but your brother Troopers. The Sheriff and his deputies will hang you out to dry in a heartbeat. The D.A. will do the same. Everybody out here is inbred and fucking each other's cousins cause they already fucked each other. We're outsiders and we always will be." After a moment of silence Big Tom continued, "You gotta watch your back and your dick. You fool around with the wrong ol bitch out here and it'll get you killed. Her last ol man will fasten a bomb to your undercarriage or hide in the brush and shoot you when you walk out your house one morning."

"Christ," Paul shifted the Sig on his hip and tasted his coffee. "Why are you still here?" He asked Big Tom, "Why haven't you rotated out?"

"Hahaha," Big Tom laughed. "I fucked up. Married a Cherokee. I love the bitch but she can't leave her family. It was all I could do to get her to move down the road from them! But what the fuck? I only got five years 'til I can retire. Then I can get serious about fishing. Raise some cows."

Paul looked out the window. Rain was beginning to fall and the vast woodland that surrounded the small town of Stilwell was turning from green to the early fall hues of burnt orange and red-brown. Their radios squawked and jabbered with static. The three men talked about college football and the internal politics of the Oklahoma Department of Public Safety. They all agreed they deserved a raise but the recent budget cut-backs made it unlikely they would receive one. The rain began to come down in sheets and the wind picked up, blowing the precipitation sideways across the diner's cracked cement parking lot. Wonderful morning for car crashes, Paul thought to himself.

The troopers paid for breakfast and went out in the rain to their cars. He should have been going off-shift but with the cut-backs they were all working mandatory nine-hour days. He drove outside of town and parked his cruiser in the driveway of a deserted house, pointing out, facing the state highway. He figured he would park there until the rain slackened or he got an emergency call. All the trees and hills, he thought, in a way it was beautiful, and then so much ugliness and eyesore in the great green midst. For the first time in over a year of living and working in eastern Oklahoma, Paul realized the truth of the country that surrounded him. Almost like a lightning strike it all fell into context. It's a ghetto, he thought, a rural ghetto. The squalor in a city was all bulldozed together on the wrong side of some railroad tracks. But out here the squalor was spread out over dozens and hundreds of square miles. Little pockets of filth, madness, crime, and vice surrounded by expanses of deep forest and green pasture. Paul pushed the intellectualization from his mind—the dispatcher was calling his unit number on the radio. There was a report of a wreck on south 59.

The OHP was an organization that ran along familial lines. Most Oklahoma State Troopers had fathers, uncles, cousins or brothers who were also state troopers. Even in a uniformed society in which nepotism was as entrenched as the OHP, Paul's uncle was a legendary and respected figure. In the mid-1990s, two convicts had escaped from a state maximum security lock-up. They had stolen some guns from a rancher's house and killed a game warden and a state trooper who crossed their felonious path. Paul's uncle was driving an unmarked cruiser and he had spotted the pair attempting to steal a car at a restaurant on the turnpike. He stealthily rolled up on the pair and caught them unawares. Without giving warning or opportunity to surrender, he had shotgunned the pair to death.

Paul thought about that sometimes. He was getting to the point where he had seen lots of dead bodies crumpled or smashed in vehicles or thrown through windshields. After a while they all ran together and failed to shock. But he wondered what it would be like to make a dead body, to produce one out of living flesh with buckshot or bullets. His uncle knew what that was like. He didn't seem bothered by it. Paul had always wanted to ask about the incident. But he could not. Such a query was an admission of weakness and state troopers don't admit weakness to themselves, much less to their mentors. That would ruin everything. A single loose thread could unravel decades of façade.

The wreck the dispatcher called him to work was a bad one. Three Cherokee kids in a Ford pickup older than they were had crossed the center line and smashed head-on into a logging truck. All the kids were dead, one wrapped around the steering wheel and two thrown out on the highway. The logging truck driver was in shock and uncommunicative. Paul went through the textbook procedures of working an accident while the volunteer firemen collected the bodies. Big Tom rolled up to assist at the accident scene. "Goddamn shame," he commented and Paul thanked God that it was raining. For some stupid reason, tears kept sneaking out of his eyes and the rain concealed the vestiges of civilian sentiment.

Tradition dictated that state troopers notify in person the next of kin when someone is killed in a motor vehicle crash. When the wrecked cars were cleaned up and loaded on tow trucks Paul and Big Tom split up the odious task. Two of the dead kids were cousins and Tom knew the family so he said he would handle those notifications. That left Paul to notify the family of Sarah Deerinwater that she was dead. He pulled out his note-filled county map to check the address. The Deerinwaters lived way out in the woods and Paul set out on the drive down the long winding gravel road to break the worst of news.

The rainstorm had slowed to a constant drizzle by the time Paul found the Deerinwater residence. It was a tiny house. Plywood and tarpaper reinforced against time and weather. A metal stovepipe jutted from one wall awkwardly, looking like it might fall. A half-dozen pickups were scattered about the yard, some with hoods up, others listing on flat tires. Paul made his face a mask and parked his car and exited the cruiser, greeted by skinny yapping dogs. The storm had moved east and he could hear the distant thunder from across the border in Arkansas. He walked across the yard, his boots descending in the muck. He knocked at the door. There was a long pause. The dogs sniffed him greedily and Paul's stomach churned as he realized they were smelling the blood on his trousers. Finally, the door cracked open and an indian woman looked out at him, avoiding his eyes. She opened the door and Paul saw the house was full of children watching T.V. and there was a man in a stained white t-shirt watching him from the kitchen's doorway. The house reeked of fried pork, wet dogs and tobacco.

"Ma'am," Paul took off his hat and held it in his right hand. He followed the script he had memorized at the Academy. "I'm State Trooper Paul Johnson. I have some very bad news. Sarah Deerinwater was killed in a traffic accident about two hours ago."

The woman's eyes widened and her face went blank and tight and she began shaking and speaking in Cherokee. The man came forward and put his arms around her. The whole house began to wail. Paul knew there was nothing more he could do, so he held out one of his business cards and said, "If there is anything I can help you with or questions I can answer please call me at anytime." But it was like they couldn't hear him. The man glowered at him behind the tears and Paul understood— he hates me, Paul thought, hates me for being white and hates me for coming to his door and fucking his world up.

No one offered to take Paul's card, so he laid it on a small table beside the door and splashed muck back to his car.

Months sped past like a drunken man in an old Cadillac, veering from boredom to sickness to terror. Paul fixated on a waitress who worked in a diner he frequented. She was younger than him and he found her very sexy in an unsophisticated country girl way. Paul thought she flirted with him but he could not tell for sure. Maybe she has a thing for men in uniforms, he thought. Her name was Christy. The pair started dating but there were not many opportunities for entertainment in Stilwell. After a couple of shabby restaurant dates the couple started holing up in Paul's rented house and ordering out for pizza.

Christy like to drink beer and smoke cigarettes and it took but little lubrication for her to gab expansively. She had dropped out of high school but had gone into a program and earned her GED. She had been a Nazi skinhead as a teenager and lived for a short while at a "white power" commune in Arkansas. Now, she regretted that phase and no longer hated blacks. She loved her mom. She had tattoos, angel wings and more, on her ankles. She offered all this up with conversational mirth. Paul listened warily but she made him smile. He was not used to drinking beer and the alcohol made him quiet and withdrawn and Christy filled in the gaps. She is lower class, Paul thought, a local yokel. But she had great legs. The curves underneath her t-shirt attracted him. Christy was completely unashamed of her emotions and when they ended up in bed together she turned submissive and eager to please.

After Paul's shift changed from graveyard to three to eleven Christy juggled her hours at the diner to approximate his and they fell into a routine of meeting at his house after their work. Christy would gab and gossip and confess while Paul listened, laughing, and tried to decompress. Soon, he gave her a key to the house and when he pulled his black and white cruiser into the driveway shortly after eleven, she would already be there, barefoot and drinking beer, preparing something to eat. "You're my man!" she'd tell him and hug him close with equal parts affection and possession. One day, Paul woke up on one of his days off and realized they were living together. He was somewhat surprised and bemused but accepted the obvious. And, in fact, he had fallen in love with her. He rationalized her past and present by telling himself she was just a small-town kid. Immature for her age but she had a good heart. And a great body.

Christy's mother was mortified that her daughter was "living in sin" with a state trooper from out of town. The two would argue for hours on the telephone while Paul tried not to listen and flipped through television channels. When Christy finally hung up on her mom she fumed and stomped through the house and popped the top on a can of beer. "Why do you go through that?" Paul asked.

"I have to. She's my mom!"

Paul just shook his head.

"Have you even told your folks about me?" Christy wanted to know.

Paul did not answer.

"You haven't? Have you?"

"No."

"Huh. Are you ashamed of me? You think I'm some white-trash bitch?"

"No, of course not. It just hasn't come up. I don't talk to my parents like you do."

"Huh. So it's OK for you to fuck my brains out but you won't tell anyone about me? I see how it is."

"Christy, come on. You know I love you. You're pissed at your mom and you're talking it out on me. Don't do that."

"Huh." Christy calmed down, "Well I want to meet your folks and I want you to meet mine."

"OK."

"You're my man and that's what I want."

"OK."

The next weekend Paul went with Christy to have Sunday dinner with her family. The house was small and cluttered and stank of decades of cigarette smoke and dogs. The siding was popping off the frame in several places and it needed a paint job. Her parents were gracious and kind and bickered with each other with obvious affection. They ate fried chicken, mashed potatoes with gravy, cornbread, and green beans. The food was good and Paul enjoyed it. When Christy went off to the bathroom her mom looked Paul straight in the eye and told him, "I don't agree with the way you kids are living but you've been good for my daughter."

Paul answered with a state-trooper issued, "Yes, Ma'am." And then he surprised himself by adding in his own voice, "I love her." Christy's mom smiled ear to ear.

Paul was parked at a rural convenience store in the dying light writing an accident report when his cell phone rang. He checked the number; it was his mother calling from Tulsa. He almost did not answer but his finger pushed the button before his brain stopped the action. "This is Trooper Johnson," he answered out of habit. "Paul?" His mother did not recognize the authoritarian tone. "Yes, Mom?"

"Paul. I have some bad news, honey."

"Yes?" Bad news was his chosen trade.

"Uncle Rick had a heart attack today."

"What?" Paul's mind jerked.

"Yes he was working an accident and he just collapsed."

"Oh no . . ."

"Yes it's real bad Paul. He's in the ICU at Saint John's."

Paul sighed. He could think of nothing to say.

"Paul are you there?"

"Yes, Mom."

"Well, I know you're real busy. I just wanted you to know. The doctor says he's stable and we're all here and praying for him."

"OK, Mom."

The phone call ended and Paul sat staring through the windshield. He discarded his accident report and shook his head. It did not make sense but of course it did. Uncle Rick was a big guy, well over six feet tall and built like a bull, but in the last decade he had added an ample gut to his frame. And, of course, he had a high-stress job and an antagonistic ex-wife. And he ate fast-food most days and dipped Skoal at work and smoked cigarettes at night. "Goddammit," Paul cursed but he shook it off, completed the report, and finished his shift.

Back at trooper headquarters Paul told Smitty and Big Tom the news and they reacted with shock and offers to cover a shift if Paul wanted to go to Tulsa and see his uncle. At first he declined their offers but then he reconsidered. If Rick did not make it, he'd feel terrible for not visiting. "No problemo," said Smitty, "You can go to Tulsa tomorrow and I'll cover the first four hours of your shift." "That's right, bro," Big Tom added, "And if you're not back by seven I'll take it from there."

"Guys, I appreciate it."

"We're family, man," Smitty told him, "We're always there for you."

Christy wanted to go with him but Paul said no, everyone was upset and it was no time for introductions. The next day he got up early and, ignoring all speed limits, drove to Tulsa. Paul had not been to the city in months and the stop and go traffic made him irritable and frustrated between the traffic lights. He had forgotten so many people existed. He parked outside the hospital and rode the elevator up to the seventh floor. The intensive care unit was full grief and concern and large men wearing the uniform of the Oklahoma Highway Patrol. Paul's mother hugged him deeply. Uncle Rick's ex-wife and teenage daughters were there and they thanked Paul for coming to the hospital. His fellow troopers, none of whom he had met before, shook his hand.

"Rick is damn proud of you," one of them told him. "He'll make it. They don't come any tougher than your Uncle Rick." Paul nodded an accepted a cup of coffee. He sat down next to his mother. She was gripping a tissue.

"It's good to see you," she told him, "I just wish it wasn't like this."

"Oh, I know. I just wanted to come."

"I'm glad you did. I don't think they will let you in cause you're not immediate family but we'll tell him you're here."

"Sure. I just wanted to come."

Paul stayed at the hospital for several hours, chatting with decorum with his mother and Rick's ex-wife and daughters. He slipped out in the hallway to grab another cup of coffee and gossip with the other troopers. He did not know any of them but already he felt more comfortable with men wearing the uniform than he did with his own family. The troopers comforted each other with snippets of black humor and white racism and by early afternoon, Paul felt his this day's mission was complete. He said his goodbyes and merged into the traffic heading east. Almost as an afterthought, he stopped at a gunshop and bought half a case of .357 Sig and two-hundred rounds of double-oo shotgun shells. Back on the highway, Paul opened up the big Crown Vic's engine, rushing back eastward between eighty and ninety miles per hour. He thought about Rick and Christy and his payroll deductions as he listened to trooper radio chatter with one ear.

An hour passed and Paul was back in the hill country, the highway turning two-lane and winding between dilapidated trailers with front yard chickens and trash piles. Out of self-defense, on these roads even he drove the speed limit. At any crossroads, an octogenarian on an antique tractor might pull out on the highway right in front of him, glaucoma-fogged eyes obscuring the black and white cruiser. Or a meth-head on a three day jag obsessing over beer at the Quick Mart might be tweaking too hard to know what lane of highway he—or she—was turning into. Paul was still half-listening to the radio chatter as he crossed the Adair County line. Suddenly, he heard Tammy, the Adair County OHP dispatcher, shrieking through the static and disregarding all procedures and codes. "Trooper down!" She was high-pitched and hysterical, "Trooper down! Twelve miles north of city limits on 59!" Paul stuck the accelerator to the floor and the heavy sedan jerked beneath him. His hands suddenly cold and shaky, he thumbed the button on his microphone and broadcast that he was responding and on the way. Jesus Christ, he thought as his car hit one-hundred-ten miles per hour on the straightaways between big curves on Highway 51. Was it Big Tom? Smitty? Fucking hell, he wanted to slap himself—my shotgun is in the trunk and I'm not wearing my vest! What the fuck? His tires were squealing through a switchback curve when his cell phone rang. He took his eyes off the road to glance at the incoming number. It was Big Tom. Paul answered, shouting over his siren. "Yeah man?"

"Where you at?"

"Four or five miles east of town. What happened?"

"Smitty got shot." Tom was yelling over his siren too. "But he's OK. He was wearing a vest. Listen . . . can you hear me?"

"Yeah, yeah."

"The perps are two Mexicans in a late eighties blue Chevy truck. They were southbound outta here."

Paul took his foot off the accelerator as his eyes locked on a blue Chevy approaching him westbound. It sailed past and Paul saw two Hispanics in the cab gesturing at each other wildly. He hit the brake and spoke into the phone. "I just met em."

"You just met em?"

"Yeah, we got em. They're westbound on 51 and I'm right behind them."

"I'm five minutes behind you. Be careful."

Paul tossed the phone into the passenger floorboard and slowed to do a three-point turnaround in a chicken farm driveway. Throwing gravel and burning rubber he spun the back tires onto the state highway in pursuit of the blue Chevy. The tuned-up interceptor engine in the Crown Vic easily caught up with the fleeing suspects. Paul stared through the windshield mind whirling as he gained ground on the Chevy and then he was right on its back bumper. The siren wailing, the red and blue lights flashing, he stayed stuck right behind the blue truck. The truck's driver accelerated to eighty, then ninety miles per hour and Paul stayed right behind them until they entered a snaking S-curve. They'll never make it through the curve at that speed, Paul thought, as he tapped the brake pedal and then stood on it, barking the tires as his sedan shook. The blue Chevy distanced out in front of him and disappeared into the curve as Paul let his cruiser coast. He forced his sedan to hug the outside shoulder and midway through the curve he saw dust rising and the guardrail smashed outward where the truck had lost control and flipped off the highway. Plumed with dust, the truck was piled up on its side, one back tire still rotating. Paul pulled off the highway behind the wreck and gave his radio report on the location. Then, he jumped out of his car with gun in hand and warily approached the crumpled Chevy.

The occupants had been thrown clear of the cab and the truck was on its side, smashing the lower two-thirds of one of them. Paul took one look at the man and knew he was looking at a corpse. The other man was staggering around through the dust and rocks, shirtless and clearly in shock. Paul pushed him to the ground and handcuffed him. In minutes, Big Tom appeared on the scene and they could hear the ambulance siren. Paul began to decompress. He realized his heart was racing and he was covered in sweat. Big Tom gave him a bear hug. "We got em Bro! We got em!"

When Paul finally made it home he found Christy frantic and beside herself with worry. She was weeping and drinking a beer. He parked his car and she was at the driver's door before he could exit.

"I've been so worried!" She hugged him tightly, "I heard a trooper got shot!"

"It's OK. I'm fine."

"Why in the hell didn't you return my calls?"

"Oh shit. I turned my phone off and forgot to turn it back on."

"What the fuck happened? I've been worried sick!"

"Smitty got shot."

"Is he dead?"

"No. He was wearing a vest. He got shot with a .22. He's gonna be fine."

Christy was still sobbing as she followed him into the house. He stripped off his gear and collapsed on the couch, exhausted. Christy brought him a beer and snuggled up against him.

"I love you so much," she said, "I don't know what I'd do if you got shot. I'd just go crazy."

"I'm not gonna get shot."

"You might. Smitty did."

"He's reckless. Doesn't follow security procedures."

Months later, the summer had burnt the green from the grass and Paul was watching cable sports with minimal interest. Christy had been quiet all day and Paul noticed she wasn't drinking beer. Out of the blue she asked him, "Do you think we'll get married?"

Paul just laughed.

"You think that's funny?"

"No."

"Then why did you laugh?"

"It's nervous laughter."

"Don't be a wise-ass. I know you're smarter than me."

"C'mon."

"Huh? What do you think?"

"Why do you bring it up?"

"Cause I think I'm gonna have a baby."

Christy was pregnant. And she and Paul got married. It was a low-key ceremony followed by a pack-and-dash honeymoon in Eureka Springs, Arkansas. Paul reserved them an actual honeymoon suite and Christy was thrilled to sit naked in a Jacuzzi and talk about their lives. Paul wanted her to quit her waitress job and think about going to college part-time. It wouldn't be hard, he told her, your mom is right by to watch the kid. Christy didn't really want to go to college. She wanted to be a momma. But she agreed with him anyway. He said he wanted her to do these things in case anything happened to him, she could make it on her own.

When the baby came, it was a boy and Christy was happy and very beautiful holding her newborn. The grandparents were all joyous and Paul stood in the maternity ward in his uniform and kissed his wife and son with a stranger's vomit on his boots.

Paul's uncle had recovered from his heart attack and retired from the Highway Patrol. He had not actually worked since his collapse on the turnpike but they had a formal retirement ceremony in Tulsa and Paul received an invitation. The ceremony was short and gruff and the Director of Public Safety presented Rick with a gold watch and a letter from the Governor and an Oklahoma flag. The troopers from Rick's office had taken up a collection and bought him a short-barreled Smith and Wesson .357 that had been customized and engraved with his name and badge number. They said it was his "retirement carry gun." Uncle Rick thanked everyone and told a few jokes. He had lost a lot of weight, Paul thought, and seemingly aged decades in months. But he was a survivor. Paul felt some pride in kinship, thinking, well, Rick gets to be an old man.

After the retirement ceremony, Paul and the rest of the troopers went over to Rick's house and cooked hamburgers on a gas grill and drank a few beers. Rick's daughters flirted shamelessly and Paul heard one of the older troopers tease his uncle, "With girls like that you're going to need a .357!"

Rick just laughed, "My girls are too smart to marry troopers. City firemen have a better benefit package."

Everyone laughed and one by one the troopers said their goodbyes and went home or to work. Paul was getting ready for the long drive back to Stilwell when Rick pulled him aside. "I want you to have some stuff," he said.

"What's that?"

"Come back here."

Paul followed his uncle to a spare bedroom and Rick handed him a rifle in a heavy plastic case.

"What's this?"

"Wilson Combat AR-15. It's yours."

"You sure?"

"I don't need it anymore. Hell, I don't want it. It's guaranteed to shoot sub-MOA but I could never get it there with my eyes."

"Wow. I don't know what it say . . ."

"Learn to use it and hope you don't have to."

"Thanks."

"And take these, too." Rick handed him a small bowling ball bag and Paul peeked inside. The bag contained several small, dusty, snubnose revolvers. Rick cleared his throat. "They may look dirty. But they're clean. Untraceable. Do you understand Bro?"

"Yes," Paul lied.

"Do what you have to. Your family needs you. That's the most important thing."

"Yes. Thanks, Rick, I don't know what to say."

"Don't say anything. Just be careful. All the time."

Paul noticed there was a cleaned and oiled semiautomatic shotgun leaning up against the wall. He stared at it for a moment and realized it was probably the shotgun Rick had used to kill those convicts years ago. I guess he's keeping that, Paul thought, the shotgun is his weapon of choice.

A year later, Christy was pregnant again and Paul finally changed his shift for 3-11 to 7-3. Now he got up at 5:00 am—it was a struggle at first, before he learned to manage his time. Christy was expecting another baby and her father was dying of cancer and they were shopping for a house to buy. He felt like he was speeding in several directions all at the same time. He looked forward to going to work most of the time because it allowed him to concentrate on the minutia and procedures of the job.

After several years of budget freeze, the state finally graduated a new class of troopers and Adair County got two of them. This eased the strain on everyone and that fall, Paul, Smitty, and Big Tom juggled their schedules and succeeded in getting the same three days off during deer hunting season. Paul had never been a hunter but Smitty was keen on the subject and Tom's mother-in-law owned three-hundred acres of scrub brush that had once been her father's farm.

They went out to the woods on a Friday afternoon with their tents, lanterns, coolers of beer and food, and rifles. The next morning, Paul could not rouse himself from his sleeping bag and despite his friends' chiding he slept in soundly. It was warm and sunny for a November day, and in the afternoon he went out to sit at the base of tree until darkness fell. He saw no deer, just jabbering squirrels and *cawcawing* birds between branches. Just before the light completely extinguished, he heard the sharp report of a rifle to his east. When he crashed back to camp amidst the hardwood leaves, Smitty was dragging a mid-sized doe, huffing and puffing and flushed from the exertion and killing. Paul helped him field-dress the animal and load it into the back of his truck. Smitty went to check it in while Paul and Big Tom worked to the keep the campfire roaring and opened cans of beer. "Get some steaks," they told Smitty before he left, "And some potatoes and aluminum foil."

Their faces reflecting flames, Paul and Big Tom snacked on cheese and crackers and drank beer. By the time Smitty made it back to camp the fire was raging and they wrapped potatoes in foil and threw them in the coals and brought out a bottle of bourbon. The alcohol stung Paul's tongue and he sipped it gently as the t-bones sizzled in the open fire. With little manner of civilization, the men ate quickly, the fire throwing their shadows onto the trees surrounding the camp. The bourbon poured again and Smitty handed out cigars and they sat in their camp chairs, feet toward the fire, laughing and telling stories. Their conversations zig-zagged from wives to guns to football. As always, they landed back discussing the job. So much to say about things they had no control over. Smitty tossed a shot down and puffed tobacco. "Man, when I got shot," he spoke across the flames and drifting smoke. "It brought all the basics back to me. What's important you know. Only one fucking thing. Coming home at the end of the day."

"That's for sure," Big Tom was slurring his words.

"I mean whatever it takes."

Paul nodded agreement, silenced by the cold air and alcohol.

"I don't give a fuck anymore," Smitty continued, "If it's a chancy, could-go-either way deal, I'm pulling the trigger. I ain't waitin around to get shot again! Man it's like when your Uncle Rick shot that nigger . . ."

Paul jerked out of his daze and flame-staring. What?, he thought, Rick did what?

". . . the passenger claimed the dude didn't have a gun and Rick threw one down but who cares? The dude made a move and Rick shot him. So what if he didn't have a gun? So what if Rick threw one down? I ain't sayin he did, you know, I'm just saying so what? There's a dead nig but Rick goes home at the end of day."

Paul found his voice. "When did that happen?"

"Right before you came out here," Big Tom said and cracked another beer. "They tried to make a big deal out of it but nothing ever happened."

"Oh," Paul settled back in his chair as the older two troopers kept talking. *It must have been while I was in the Academy.* He thought back on those sixteen weeks of hell. No T.V., no newspapers, just up every morning at 5:30 to run and study and shoot and drive. Paul dropped his chin closer to his chest and pulled the brim of his cap down to block the bright flames. I can't believe no one ever mentioned it to me. Rick had been involved in a suspicious shooting and no one ever said a word about it. They wanted to protect me, he told himself. Was that it? Christ what a fucking deal. Paul's mind whirled through the haze of bourbon. And when Rick gave me those beater snubnose revolvers? Paul's psyche stuttered through the implications. What was that? A threat? A warning? An insurance policy via the network of related state troopers? Had Rick shot an unarmed man? Paul heard his uncle's words like a bell ringing in his memory: "Do what you have to—you have a family to protect." Paul shook it off and forced himself to laugh at a story Big Tom was telling. He heard his own laughter as bitter and hollow.

The whiskey helped him sleep soundly without dreaming and Paul awoke well before dawn and crawled out of his tent into the cold air. Beer cans were littered around the fire and he could hear his friends snoring deeply. He wrapped himself in layers of clothing and climbed into a tree stand to await the deer of morning. Just after daybreak, a small herd appeared out of the brush, browsing to and fro, and Paul shot the largest doe using the Wilson AR his uncle had given him. Smitty helped him field-dress the deer and urged him to smile while posing for a picture with his trophy. "That's a fine deer," Smitty told him, "She'll taste good for you."

The second baby was a girl and Paul and Christy bought a house just outside of Stilwell. Her father beat the cancer then relapsed and died a week after their daughter's first birthday. "I don't know why the cancer got him," Christy said and her mom guessed it was God's will. Paul held his daughter in his lap and did not mention the years of cigarette smoking. They don't understand cause and effect, he noted to himself. He just kept quiet and let them grieve.

The funeral was Southern Baptist and emotional. I can't let my kids grow up out here, Paul thought. By the time they go to school we've got to get the fuck out of here. But they had a house they were paying off and he knew Christy could never live far from her mother. The preacher spoke behind the open casket and Paul sat thirty feet and a thousand miles away. I fucked up, he realized. I married a local.

The kids were napping and Christy was making chili, barefoot, with a beer can held balanced on her hip. "You never talk anymore," she said, "I don't know why."

"I don't know what to say."

"Say anything. What did you do today?"

"Wrote some tickets and arrested a drunken indian."

"Was it exciting?'

"It was depressing."

"Do you still love me?"

"Yes."

"Well I love you too. And the babies love their Daddy. And I'm proud of you. You're a good man."

"That's nice to hear."

After they ate, Christy's mom came over to watch the kids and Paul and Christy went to Wal-Mart and bought groceries and diapers and socks. "Your birthday is coming up," she told told him, "What do you want?"

Paul laughed, "You don't have to get me anything."

"Yes I do! And the babies want to get you something!"

"They don't know."

"Yes, they do—I told them."

"Well, I'm sure anything you pick out would be nice."

"How bout this?" Christy pulled a gaudy faux cowboy shirt off the rack.

"Not that, please." They both laughed and wheeled their carts to the checkout line.

In eastern Oklahoma, the weather changes quickly and people say the forecasts are as often as not inaccurate. Winter days can be sunny and the temperature rises toward sixty degrees and then an ice storm blows in from the western plains and the next day the temperature plummets to below freezing and the roads turn impassable beneath the frozen precipitation. In summer, the morning and afternoon will be still with blue sky stretching in every direction. Then, as the sun goes to rest the clouds gather and the wind picks up and a thunderstorm erupts with like cannon-burst sheets of rain blowing sideways. Paul worked through and around the weather; it did not matter to him anymore. From where he sat in his cruiser, it looked like clouds were gathering on the western horizon but he paid them no mind. He was parked in front of his favorite rural convenience store's parking lot writing an accident report. He stretched the process to kill time and when no new calls came across his radio he ended his shift and drove home. He walked in the door and read Christy's note—she had run to her mom's house and would be back soon. He took off his gunbelt and uniform and was stretching out in front of the T.V. when his cellphone rang. It was his mother and she was sobbing. "Paul! Something terrible has happened."

He felt the blood pressure increase in his wrists, "What happened?"

"Paul . . . Uncle Rick shot himself."

"What?'

His mother was barely in control of herself, "Paul he's dead."

Paul's mind spun like a rotating tire throwing gravel before catching pavement, "When did this happen?"

"This afternoon. Dear God it must've been an accident. He must have been cleaning the shotgun when it went off . . ."

Paul bit his tongue until the pain allowed him to lie. He knew Rick was an expert handler of firearms. If he shot himself it was on purpose. "Yes, Mom, it must have been an accident." He breathed deep. "It's a terrible accident." He listened to his mother crying and they spoke for a few more minutes. He ended the call as Christy came into the house, the screen door banging behind her and the children shrieking for Daddy.

The funeral was full of state trooper stoics with black armbands sitting in straight rows. Paul sat with the family as they lowered the casket into the ground. Rick's shock-strewn daughter hugged him, sobbing. They both told him how proud Rick had been of his nephew and he heard his aunt remark on how much he resembled his suicided uncle. It's the uniform, he told himself, and the close-shorn haircut. Then he remembered shaving that morning and the emergence of his first grey hairs.

It began raining that afternoon as Paul, Christy, and the children drove back east from the funeral in Tulsa. His son slept like a rock in the backseat of the cruiser but his daughter was a wailer. Paul tuned her out and focused on the highway, driving fast, as always. He said nothing, stared straight where the big car was aiming, fixated on the highway, overcompensating for grief on the minutia of driving fast in the rain. Finally, his daughter settled down and fell asleep and when Paul glanced over to the passenger seat, Christy was looking out beyond the windshield wipers with tears streaming down her face.

A few months later, Smitty was sick with the flu and Paul was covering his shift. Sixteen hours in a cruiser with the last eight hours at time and a half. Paul was parked on a gravel shoulder facing oncoming traffic on the state highway. Vehicles would come over the hill and see him sitting there and invariably they would tap their brakes in response. Paul was not even bouncing the radar, he was just sitting there maintaining a presence, he told himself. The vehicles roared by and the sun was setting. How much more, Paul wondered, and for the hundredth time he ran the numbers in his head. Fifteen years minimum until retirement. Hundreds of accidents and thousands of tickets. Dozens of family notifications. Hundreds of arrests and thousands cups of coffee.

Thirteen years to pay off the mortgage. More years of everything. How much more? It twisted his gut to consider. It's a stupid bitter joke, he thought. And there was a time I wanted it all so bad. Wanted the job and wanted Christy and now my lungs are in such a vise I can't hardly breath. An 18-wheeler shuddered past, his cruiser rocking in its wake. He stared into the lights on the dashboard until they grew blurry, then he blinked hard to focus and took a sip of coffee. The truth was, he put on a uniform and went out in the morning and nothing good could happen. He almost laughed at the absurdity. All that matters is going home at the end of the day. His radio crackled to life—there was a bad wreck on south 59.

RANDALL'S TALE

Nobody wanted to sell any land to a bunch of hippie-freaks. They didn't want us as neighbors. It was right after that T.V. movie about Manson came out and I guess they thought we wuz killers. We finally found a blind lawyer and bought this place from him. He probably conned some poor indian out of it. The plan wuz to have an anti-nuke and music commune and build geodesic domes to live in. That wuz a long time ago. Now I know—domes leak and communes don't work. But we had good times, great parties. Once this indian friend of mine came back from Taos with a shoebox full of peyote. We all ate some and got all tripped out and then he got pissed at me cause I wouldn't follow the ritual. Ah man, I never liked rules, I didn't want to do no chanting, I jus wanted to play my Stratocaster.

I built this little dome first, about fourteen feet in diameter. One night, while we were wuz at the Rainbow Gathering in Missouri, they came and shot it full of holes. Cowboys, scared of hippies. They tried to burn us out but

I guess it started raining. You know the wild thing? They came on horses. Horses! They left tracks all over the place. We didn't know what to do, talked about it, you know. Then we took a couple of rifles and backtracked em three miles through the woods. Followed those tracks all the way to ol Gruver's corral. They said he was a bad man and I guess he didn't like hippies. We didn't know what to do, wondered if we should settle it the Cherokee County way you know? But then we thought, no, we're not that kind of men. We walked away. I guess we made the right call cause six months later Gruver's own cousin shot him through the belly at his mother's house on Labor Day. Then he walked over an put another bullet in his head. Judge says, 'First bullet is free, but the second one will cost you ten years.' I think he only done about five though.

Yeah, it was terrible, before we opened that road on the ridge line we had to come up this hill. If you weren't doing sixty at the bottom you'd never make it up. Then it took me years to cut that road. I don't even know how many chainsaws I destroyed. I made every mistake you can possibly make cutting down trees. I almost got killed so many times it's a wonder I'm still alive. Finally we got that road through there but it was really only a trail. I'd get a van stuck up to the axles in there and then the rain would start to freeze. I'd hike up there the next morning and limbs and trees woulda been broken down in the ice storm blocking the van that was stuck in the mud. Couldn't cut though em cause I wuz outta chainsaw oil. Couldn't go get chainsaw oil cause my van was stuck in the mud. It went on like that for years. I swear 'fore God I paved that road with transmissions and axles. I tore up eight vehicles tryin to get through on that road. Finally Puckett felt sorry for me and gave me that '63 one-ton. I geared it down and at least I could pull myself outta the mud. Then, after sixteen years, the county came out here and graded it. I don't know why. I'd been tryin to get them to do it for years and finally they did. I mean it's supposed to be a county road anyway, I guess it wuz back in the fifties. Now it's pretty much completely gone between me and Cricket. Nuthin more than a deer-trail. He comes in from the north and I come in from the south. I hadn't seen him in six years and then we wuz playin at the Woody Guthrie Folk Festival and these young hippies and I wuz having a rap session on eco revolution and up walks Cricket. We only live a mile apart but we had to drive two hours to Okemah just to see each other and say hi.

All I ever wanted to do wuz live in the woods and make a livin playin fiddles and guitars. I never wanted to be an automotive mechanic but I've had to turn into one just to get in and outta here. I've had ever type of automotive breakdown you can possibly imagine. I've broke axles, dropped transmissions, had wheels spin plumb off, replaced dozens of alternators, generators and carburetors, had radiators explode, steering wheels come off in my hands. Lord, it's just a wonder I'm alive after all the automotive problems I've had. One night I was coming back from a session job in Austin and as soon as I turned onto our road all the motor mounts snapped and the engine fell right outta the van. That wuz a mess. Another time I'd been huntin hard all season. Built a little dome huntin blind and been sittin in there day after day. Seen hide nor hair of deer the whole time. The last day of season the sun went down and I just gave up and went to the store for beer. I'm drivin down the trail and Bang! Crash! Boom! A deer jumped right through the passenger window and starts thrashin around and beatin me all to hell. That wuz terrible. I lost control of the car and drove head-on into a tree. It's a wonder I'm still alive after that. I had a smashed car, a concussion, and two broken fingers. Couldn't play music for two months. That wuz the most expensive deer-meat I never brought home.

I haven't had a job since I was twenty-two. I've been playing music full-time for almost forty years. It's amazing how little money I've made. It just amazes me. If it weren't for squirrel and catfish I woulda starved to death a long time ago. But the truth is, I've about lost my taste for squirrel. Now, I just wanna eat raw foods. I've been eatin a pound of nuts every day and a half pound of fruit. I feel great! Feel better now than when I wuz forty years old. Course I ain't takin the cocaine no more. Every day is a new day. I ain't got much but I don't want much. Just wanna write songs and play with my bands. I've been collecting maps, trying to find an all-water route from Spring Creek to New Orleans. I got a little boat and I'd like to float all the way down like they did in the old days. The problem is all the damn dams. I'm still workin on it.

REDNECKS IN CONVERSATION

"We had a sheriff here one time a-name of Johnson and he only lasted one term."

"He wasn't very popular huh?"

"No he wasn't. He was the kinda sheriff that would take you to the jailhouse for takin a deer outta season."

"Yeah?"

"Christ I was a full-growed man for I even knew a deer took a tag. My Daddy an uncles kilt deer year-round. They raised cows for money and shot deer for food."

"That's wut they did innit?"

"After my Daddy passed my uncle Bob told me when they was young men an I was a baby they kilt a deer in winter down on the river and they was dressin it out when game warden came by and made a ruckus bout it. Uncle Bob said Daddy had a pistol in his coat pocket and a .30-.30 leanin up against a tree. The game warden told em to step away from the deer and put their hands up and Daddy snatched that .30-.30 and levered it and aimed it right at the warden's head. Bob said the game warden froze up and Daddy told him just to go into town and have a cup of coffee cause he's jus as soon kill a man as go to jail over deer-meat. And the warden just walked away.

"Really?"

"That's what uncle Bob said and I never knew him to tell a lie. I never seen my Daddy act like that but there's lots of things I don't know about him. He never liked to talk on himself."

MUSKOGEE, 1919

from the remembrance of Cecilia Jamison

. . . yes'm my Daddy started the negro Church of the First Born an he used to reckon he was the only man who coulda taken the old ways to the negroes livin around Muskogee. He'd go on to say that the Lord had chose him for the work cause he knew the ways of our people and the injuns equal as well.

You see they mis-took Daddy's Ma an Pa fer injun cause they both had more than a lil Comanch in em. So when they's dividin up the land there for statehood Grandma an Pa got em an allotment there in Lincoln County and Daddy growed up there amongst the Iowa injuns an learnin their ways of speakin an other ways as well. An so by the time Daddy was a growed man he could speak Iowa and Pawnee an Comanch purt near as well as anyone who weren't born to it could. An that's when he took the peyote the first time. They wuz havin a meetin there in the Nation an Daddy told me many times how he rode a plow mule most of the day cause he wanted to go to the meetin cause he'd heard all about em.

The young bucks thereabouts the meetin place didn't like Daddy bein there cause of him bein a negro. They didn't want a black man takin up the ol injun religion. But the ol injuns, the elders, said it wuz alright. They told em Father Peyote is the father of the negros same as he's the father of the injun. So Daddy took peyote for the first time that way and he'd take it many times after that. They'd eat the Old Man and smoke him as well. An Daddy learnt the ways of Father Peyote there amongst them injuns. He learnt things no other negros ever did know.

Right around the turn of the century one of Christ's shepherds came through the Nations reviving folks left an right and baptizing them in the name of Jesus. Daddy took the faith then and got hisself baptized. The Holy Ghost came on Daddy something fierce and he started testifyin all over the Creek Nation actin as one a Christ's shepherds hisself an preachin and healin folks both injun an negro. An for many years he did this sides his farmin. All the time we kids wuz growin up purt near every week Daddy would go out an revive folks. Mama told us how proud we should be of our Daddy as he could see things other men couldn't see an then preach it out to all that would listen. That's the kinda man Daddy wuz. A shepherd for Jesus jus like John or Paul in the Good Book. An our neighbors knowed it too. Many wuz the time they'd bring us a he-goat or a pair of layin hens. We wuz poor negros but we didn't know that we wuz poor.

Along there in the spring of 1919 wuz when Daddy had the first meetin that wuz equal parts Old Ways and Good Book. He had it there on the old farm place and in particular in the barn. Daddy made us girls stay in the house but we seen him put on his chief's feathers and blanket that wuz his grandpas. He'd already took the

Epsom salts and hot bath the night before, on account he said he'd see spooks and crazy things iffins he didn't.

An it weren't long fore I got to attend the meetins myself. We'd sit in circle in the barn, burn sage an cedar in the smoke pit along with the medicine feathers and cane. The womens sat on the left of Daddy and the mens sat on the right. We sat like goats, on our heels an we'd sing and clap along wit the drum. Along at midnight after we'd passed the sacred bowls of food around we'd eat of Father Peyote. Daddy would say a prayer an then he'd recite scripture. At the same time one of the mens would shape the fire-ashes into the shape of a heart. After finishin his scripture Daddy would stamp on the fire an ashes an smooth it all out with his feet. By then Father Peyote would be talkin loud in our heads and as the drum beat slow-like we all be quiet and listen to what the Old Man wuz sayin. A pipe of cedar would pass around and we'd all smoke deep. One of the mens would make a new fire then an when it wuz roarin we'd all start to sing and sing.

Many times folks would take a healin there when we wuz singin. Other times somebody would start to chant out what the Old Man wuz saying. We'd jus sing along no matter. That wuz the testifyin you see, the singin.

All night we'd sing together. Then at dawn Daddy would throw open the bard door an we'd all stand an hold hands an sing, "Till We Meet Again." When the sun hit the center of the fire the meetin wuz over and we'd go sit in the grass an eat sweet corn and roasted beef.

For seven years that's the way it wuz. An even tho the law got nosy an sent deputies to poke around we didn't pay em no mind. The things that cain't be seen, that's what we listened to. Cause everything you can see, sure-nuff it belongs to someone else.

MUSKRAT'S TALE

I opened the door and saw two white men in suits with badges I could read well enough: their IDs said FBI. I hollered to my wife in Cherokee, "Come out here and tell these FBI agents I can't speak English!" And she did a great job of it. Waving her arms, calling them racists, a real crazy squaw routine. And it worked. They left. The next week they came back with a Cherokee Nation Marshal. I didn't know the guy but I knew who he was. He could speak very little Cherokee but tried to play it off like he was fluent. Again they knock on the door. And I holler at my wife and she comes out again going crazy on em. 'We brought an interpreter,' the one agent says, 'who speaks Cherokee. We want to interview your husband.' My wife goes absolutely ape-shit. 'You dumb-ass white boys,' she's screaming at them, 'Just cause my ol man can't speak English don't mean he speaks Cherokee! He speaks Mvskoke! You racist crackers think all indians speak one language!' Now the feds are confused and the marshal looks real relieved. Of course, the Marshal knows who I am and knows I'm Cherokee but there are a handful of Cherokees who grew up in traditional Creek towns and speak Mvskoke. So the Marshal thinks it's bullshit but it's not entirely impossible. They leave and my wife and I laugh and laugh.

The next week they come back in two cars. Three FBI agents get out and they have the Cherokee Nation Marshal with them and a Creek Nation Lighthorse officer. 'Here we go again,' I tell my wife and she rushes out of the house like a crazy woman. The older FBI agent, the one who hadn't been at the house before stops her and tells her real seriously. 'Ma'am we know your husband can speak English. We have a recorded telephone call between him and a federal fugitive and he is most definitely speaking English.' Then he turns to me. 'Joe just answer some of our questions. No more bullshit. Please?' I look at him like I have no fucking idea what he is saying. My wife goes off again, 'Whoever you have on tape speaking English it's not my husband. Because he don't speak English! Never have! Never will!'

The older agent is trying to stay calm and reason with my wife and he asks her, 'What language do you and your husband speak in your home?' And my wife, god bless her, is smart as hell. She looks at the Cherokee Marshal and she looks at the Creek Lighthorse officer and she tells him, 'We speak Mvskoke. The Yuchi dialect thereof.' Hahaha. I see the Lighthorse officer's disappointment. Cause maybe he can speak Mvskoke and maybe not. Most likely he speaks some but very little. But no way can he speak the Yuchi dialect of Mvskoke because there is no such thing. A fluent Mvskoke speaker might understand one Yuchi word out of forty cause a little of it crossed over. But my wife, God bless her, was willing to bet on the lighthorse ignorance. And it worked. And the older FBI agent says, 'Ma'am can you translate so we can ask your husband a few questions and get answers and we can stop bothering you?' Of course I speak English and Spanish and Cherokee and Mvskoke and some Yuchi. But my wife speaks English and Lakota and a little bit of Cherokee she picked up from me. And I know maybe fifty words of Lakota but not enough to talk it really.

So my wife asks me in Lakota if I am willing to be interviewed with her acting as interpreter. And, just for the hell of it, I answer in the little bit of Navajo I know, 'Sure why not?' She has no idea what I'm saying but she takes it as a yes and the interview begins. I listen to the FBI's questions in English and wait for my wife to translate it into Lakota (which we are pretending is Yuchi dialect Mvskoke) and then I answer in Yuchi plus a pidgin of western indian words I start throwing together for fun. They want to know if I am a member of A.I.M. and I say yes. They want to know if I know Peltier and Trudell and the usual suspects and my wife answers honestly on my behalf, yes, I know all of them. How well do I know them, the FBI inquires and I rattle on for a while wondering how my wife will answer this one. 'How well could he know them?' she asks the agents, 'He doesn't speak English! He's been in the same room with them and they drank beer but as I'm sure you can understand there was a little communication problem!' And then they ask about the dude they are really interested in. I'm not even gonna use his name. But he was a Weather Underground alumni. Connected to the Black Liberation Army. A fugitive with heavy felony warrants. Yes, I knew him. We had hid him for a while when he was moving across the country in the underground. We helped him get to Central America where he joined the Sandinistas. He's probably dead now. But we never talked on the phone. He would not have done a thing like talking on a phone and neither would I. My wife 'translates' this question and I go yadda yadda and she tells them, 'No he doesn't know the dude.'

The FBI agents don't believe this and they challenge us on it. 'Why would he know this guy?' my wife asks. 'My husband hates white people!' They repeat that they have a recording of me and the fugitive speaking on the phone and wife rolls her eyes. She didn't even have to do any acting cause this was total bullshit. 'My husband doesn't talk on phones,' she told them, 'Ever. Who the fuck would he talk to that speaks Yuchi dialect Mvskoke?' They go on to ask about some other people I honestly knew nothing about and then they left. We never saw them again and that's good because my understanding is it's a fairly serious federal felony to lie to FBI agents.

JUNE'S TALE

When I think about Grandpa, I can only think about
the old man I knew. In a wheelchair, both legs gone
beneath the knee, smoking a cigarette. He smelled bad. I
was scared of him, a city girl, going with my parents to
visit in the country. It was just a different world, dirty,
smoky, strange smells. There were chickens and a pig.
They had dogs that I was interested in playing with but
they weren't friendly dogs. I remember looking in the
storm shelter and pretending it was a cave. I remember
my dad taking me to the creek and grandma and my aunt
wearing those old-time dresses. I remember Grandpa
pulling me aside one time, I must have been ten or
eleven, with a twinkle in his eye he told me, "I killed two
niggers in 1947." That really terrified me. He had said it
like it was a special joke he told only on holiday
occasions.

On the way back to Tulsa, I told my dad what grandpa
had said and he got all upset and told me it wasn't true.
"He was just trying to make a bad joke," Dad told me,

"and people like us don't use that kind of language. It's a sign of ignorance. He's an old man, Junie, you have understand his mind's not right."

When grandpa died a few years later I remember the funeral as cold and rainy. Not in any town. I remember the cemetery as being surrounded by miles of forbidding forest as seen out a car window. I was worried about my father, he seemed very upset and weakened. After they lowered the casket he hugged me for one of the very few times I can recall. He sobbed. It was shocking to me. I was scared.

I went to visit grandma less and less frequently as my high school and college years went by. I thought about Keota less and less.

If I had hadn't forgotten what grandpa told me that day, I at least had not thought about it for twenty-five years. Grandma outlived her husband by several decades and when she died, I was helping my dad go through her things to get the old house and property for sale. The house had really deteriorated over the years and we were both kind of staggered to see what disrepair it was really in. "I can't believe she was living like this and I didn't know," Dad told me. He was ashamed. And it was pretty bad, filth, dust, rat droppings. In a trunk I found various old papers and documents. I also found a patina-flecked badge and rusty Colt revolver. I read through some of the papers and found out grandpa had been town marshal of Keota from 1942 to 1949. I thought back to his story. Was it true he had killed two black people?

I was stunned. Maybe he had. Was my grandpa a murderer? The gun and badge seemed to give credence to his claim. I didn't say one word to my dad about it. I didn't want to.

I thought about all of this for a long time. Grandma was dead, my aunts were dead. Dad didn't know any more about it than I did. I tried to do some research but didn't learn anything. Then my daughters came along and for a long time I was just in survival mode. I forgot about it mostly.

TIM'S TALE

I have memorized the names and social security numbers of the shooters who did the work on 19 April. They were members of the "Hostage Rescue Team." They shot the people as they tried to run out of the burning buildings. They fired their rifles in three-shot bursts, like the professionals that they are, not wasting ammo at the high point of their careers. I have seen the photos of the children, they were in a special hiding place underground. This hiding place had no ventilation, and as the FBI pumped the building full of CS gas, the children had no place to go. The CS gas rigidified and contorted their muscles, and the photos show some of the children folded backwards like pretzels. Their spines snapped by the force their muscles were exerting.

The events of that day have altered every facet of my life. Nothing would ever be the same.

I remember a few days before the massacre, it would have been the forty-something day of the standoff or "siege." I was in a hotel room in Nebraska, about a quarter mile from a truck stop off I-80. I was listening to a shortwave radio show; the speaker was broadcasting live via sat-phone from Waco. He said he could see the Branch-Davidian compound lit up by FBI spotlights through his field glasses. I will never forget what he said. The static was heavy, the sound was fading in and out. He said, "If the citizens of this country don't start arriving here immediately with arms, the government is going to burn these people alive!" Still, I couldn't believe it was true a few days later when I watched it happen. I spent the day glued to the T.V., watching the replays and news conferences and official expert explanations. I had no way of knowing that day how my life was changing. I didn't hear the doors slamming shut. All I felt was a tugging at my sleeve.

I was born during the first week of the Tet Offensive, 1968. I grew up in western Pennsylvania. My parents divorced when I was seven and I grew up living with my Dad. Dad works in a cardboard factory; he has all his life. I love my Dad but there was always this separation between us. I could never look up to him. He always seemed soft, like he had been crushed by his life and losing Mom. But he was a good Dad, he just never knew what to tell me.

The last thing I wanted was to work in a factory for the rest of my life but I didn't know what to do. Now, I think I should have gone to college and been a lawyer or historian. But that just wasn't on the table. I didn't even have the conception that going to college was possible. No one ever mentioned it to me. I liked guns and camping so I joined the army.

I started reading in the army. I read about 1775 and the Civil War and about Jefferson and the assassination of Kennedy. I began to see the lies I had been told in school. It happened a little bit at a time. I was a good soldier in the Gulf. I killed a lot of people. Once we hit a bunker with a wireless rocket. The Iraqi soldiers came running out firing all over the place. I was on a scoped .50 mounted on a Humvee and as they rushed out into the desert I started taking their heads off at 1500 yards. My LT was looking through his field glasses and he couldn't believe it, headshot, headshot, headshot, at 1500 yards.

Sometimes kids came up to us and begged for food. They wouldn't let us give them any and it bothered me a lot.

My company got back to the States and the LT asked me if I wanted to go to Special Forces school. I was pretty out of shape and burnt from the War but I said why not, I'll go through the qualification course. So they sent me to Ft. Benning to get up at dawn and run and take IQ tests. One morning before breakfast, they lined us up in front of the barracks and a Captain read out seven or eight guys' social security numbers. Mine was one of the numbers read out. The class went to breakfast and those of us singled-out, stayed. Next, a Lieutenant Colonel shows up and he and the Captain call us into a room with donuts and coffee, then give us this vague presentation about "Opportunities other than exist in the regular army." This is the way it happens, I thought, I'm being recruited to do contract work for the CIA. I filled out their forms—it took most of the day. But I never heard from them again. Four days later I sprained both ankles on an obstacle course. They swelled up the size of softballs. No way could I go on like that, so I dropped out of the qualification course. I went back to my Company but I was growing more and more disillusioned with the army. I was tired of saluting assholes for the privilege of killing people for the bankers and Wall Street.

I came home to Pennsylvania and got a job as a security guard. I worked all night and covered my windows with cardboard so I could sleep during the day. I continued reading history and I bought a shortwave radio and listened to what I heard. I took notes and did my own research. I began to see there were no accidents in American history. When they usurped the Constitution, they did it for a reason. They want to bring in a one-world police state. For the first time, I regretted killing all those Iraqis. I had been sent to do it to bring in a New World Order. Some people call it ZOG, Zionist Occupied Government, but it is more than just some Jews. It is secret societies and bankers and the military industrial complex. They work together to bring in a New World Order. All of this began to drive me crazy. Grandpa saw it. He never knew why, but one day I showed up at his door, freezing outside, in only sweats and a t-shirt. I was near total complete breakdown. Grandpa, I'm sure, never told anybody about that day and I respect him greatly for that. I spent about an hour at his house, losing it. I was almost suicidal at that point. Rage, denial, acceptance—all those feelings were battling for control.

I quit my job and drove cross-country to Waco during the siege. The things I learned there and the people I met convinced me of the unmistakable truth. The country in which I was a citizen was becoming totalitarian. In the face of such a situation there are only two options: acceptance or resistance. I chose the latter.

I realized there would be no justice for the people murdered at Waco. The killers would never be punished for their crimes. I continued traveling around the country, going to gun shows. I'd be on some interstate in Kansas, a trunk full of t-shirts, books, and used guns. I'd think about Waco, and how, after they burnt the building to the ground, they raised the American flag over the ruins. It made me want to scream. I'd go to the next gun show and set up my wares on a table. I remember one time I sold a Chinese AK-47 to a guy who was there with his wife. They had their kid with them in a stroller. After the bought the rifle, he told me "I don't care how many bodies we have to step over, it's time to take this country back!" It made me smile—I was proud to be selling him a rifle.

I started meeting people who were forming militias. They were from Michigan, Oklahoma, Ohio, Arizona, from all over. They were my kind of people, average guys who loved guns and freedom. A lot of them reminded me of my Dad but they weren't broken down by the years in the factory or mill. They still had their ideals intact. I stayed in some of their houses, drank beer with them after gun shows. We all agreed that the government had been taken over by thieves and fascists. The militia guys were waiting for the Feds to do a gun grab or declare martial law. Then they were going to head for the hills or go underground. They weren't talking about politics or even revolution, they were talking about a civil war.

Waco continued to smolder for a lot of us. We knew what had happened there. Forget, no way. Forgive, never. I hooked up with a couple of army buddies from before the war. One lived in Arizona and the other in Ohio. I worked the gun show circuit all through the Midwest, crashing on my buddics' couches on either side of the cycle. We had all woken up, we knew what was going on. We started preparing to exercise our hatred. It was not blind, it was sensible. The rifles, my Glock, the backpacks, boots, camo, radios, water purifiers, ammunition, the maps—it was all sensible. I decided I didn't want to live in one of their concentration camps, that I'd rather bleed to death in the Ozarks. That is what they have in store for those who do not accept the New World Order. I've read Hegel, I know the theorem. Thesis plus antithesis equals synthesis. We set up a system of caches for our guns and goods in different National Forests. We were ready for the shit to happen, ready to go. But the clock kept moving, *tick, tick, tick*.

"How long are we going to wait?" I would ask people, "How far are we going to let them push us?" No one had a good answer for how the civil war would start. "We need at least ten years to prepare a ground war," Mark from Michigan told me and then he added, with his eyes twinkling, "but we may not wait that long."

My friends and I decided not to wait.

I don't hate the blacks because they're fooled and fucked over just like everybody else. I don't even hate the Jews but they are not going to be able to keep all that they've stolen. I don't know who I hate because you never see their faces. The lackeys who wear the uniforms are only worthy of contempt. I don't even consider them human, not like my Mom or Sister or Grandad.

We had to try to start the civil war and maybe some day it will be understood. The government had to be told they couldn't just burn people alive and walk away. That there would be a price. That some of us would pay them back in blood. Man for man, woman for woman, child for child. I am not sorry and I have no regrets for what we did. I am an American patriot and I am prepared to die.

LA HARPE AMONGST THE INDIANS
1718

The king of France gave La Harpe a grant to trade with the indians along the Red River and after much exploration he found an excellent spot in the river's big bend. A canebrake stretched for miles and ended in a growth of strong timber which surrounded a luxuriant prairie. The river was fordable at low water along this bend where it had a hard rocky bottom. A perfect location from which to trade and hold council with the savages, thought La Harpe, and, after negotiation, he purchased the great bend from an elderly Nassonite chief. They bartered with only half-interest. He had no use for the bend in the river, he told LaHarpe, but he would much like guns and cloth and hatchets. In due time a deal was struck: thirty muskets, twelve bolts of cloth and nine hatchets. The chief went away happy and La Harpe set about the work of building a cabin.

At various intervals, indians came to visit La Harpe. Always they were full of gossip and wanting gifts. They told the Frenchmen of Spaniards and buffalo and intrigues large and small among the neighboring tribes.

Some trading was done but La Harpe received nothing of much value. Eventually translators and assistants came up the river to join La Harpe's post, and in the spring of 1719 he felt well-enough ensconced to go journeying about the country. He sent his corporal, Du Rivage, with presents aplenty to search out the Anadarkos who were said by all to possess many horses and to be a people who traded fairly.

After many weeks Du Rivage returned with two dozen horses and much information. "All the savage nations are eager to meet with you," He told LaHarpe, "They despise the Spanish who take their boys as slaves and will not sell them arms."

"Excellent," La Harpe rubbed his bearded chin with anticipation. In Du Rivage's absence, two negro servants had come up the river with letters for their new master. La Harpe explained to the corporal that France and Spain were now at war. And that their mission amongst the indians was now of great importance to their superiors in New Orleans. "If the savages can be brought under the banner of our king," La Harpe explained, "the Spaniards northern advance can be held in check."

With a sense of urgency, preparations were made to go forth and hold council with the indians. Pack saddles were constructed and the horses were trained to carry them. Friendly indians were employed to interpret and act as guides. Trade goods and presents were amassed. All summer such activities occupied La Harpe and his company. As the grass began to wither, they moved out west. La Harpe, Du Rivage, four soldiers and two indians rode in single file. Behind them the pack horses followed, tethered together. The two negros brought up the rear of the column. Mounted bareback on burros, they urged the horses forward when the laden beasts faltered.

The company traversed westward with use of compass through strong stands of timber, meadows and vine-criss-crossed underbrush. For fourteen days, they journeyed, occasionally killing deer or turkeys for sustenance. La Harpe was greatly pleased with the country. It appeared to him abundant.

The morning of the seventeenth day, a party of Nassonite warriors came to join the expedition. The Nassonites had been hunting and they claimed to have killed twenty-six buffalo and to be carrying the choice cuts. But now they were anxious to return to their village. They had heard volleys of gunfire in the hills and feared Osage. La Harpe attempted to assuage their fears but they seemed unconvinced. They told LaHarpe horror stories of Osage depredation. The Nassonites and the French traveled together for two days. Then they each went their own way.

One morning La Harpe spied a unicorn in the underbrush. The beast bolted, bounding into the curtain of forest.

"My god!" La Harpe jerked his head around to shout at Du Rivage, "Did you see that soldier?"

"Yes!"

Most certainly he had seen the mythical leap into flesh. Around the campfire after darkness, the Frenchmen spoke of such wonders. Of treasure beyond belief. Of savage aboriginal rites. Of women, both here in the wilderness and those left in Europe. Of martial tales. Of dreams.

On the twenty-fourth day they encountered a band of savages—the Osage—who approached them brazenly on the trail. Although officially friends with the French, La Harpe knew that they could be treacherous. The friendly indians in the expedition wanted to flee but La Harpe, Du

Rivage and the soldiers did not flinch as the Osage grew near. "Prepare your weapons but make no offense!" La Harpe shouted the order and placed his hand on his sword. Each Osage warrior stood as a colossus, a head and shoulder taller than the Europeans and Africans. The Osage kept their weapons in hand. The lack of fear displayed by the French must have pleased the indians since they halted, making hand signals and speaking bewilderment upon LaHarpe's ears. A negro translator came forward to whisper toward La Harpe, "They want to smoke, Sir."

"Very well!" The wilderness ambassador was pleased with the fine show his party displayed for these indians and, smiling, he looked upon the Osage as he told them and the translator, "Tell them we wish to retire and smoke the pipe. That we are French. We come to make no war unless attacked." The Osage knew they were French and their headman spoke through the negro interpreter, "Our people are friends and we wish no trouble with you. But your guides there, those lesser indians, would you take offense if we killed them and took their scalps?"

La Harpe listened seriously. He glanced at Du Rivage who displayed no change of countenance. Their guides were terrified and would give first thought to fleeing rather than fighting. Should they risk a fight? After brief consideration La Harpe made an appeal to honor. "They are our guides in this country," La Harpe explained. "We can not give them up as we are traveling together as friends. We wish warfare never unless it is against the Spanish. We wish to be friends and trade with all the indians."

The Osage seemed disappointed but did not press the issue. The pipe was brought out and smoked intently, passing from hand to hand, the men mostly silent and observing each other closely. The Osage asked what the French carried as presents. Many things of value, La Harpe assured them, and the Osage wished to see the items. The negro was told to shout for a bundle to be taken off a mule and brought forward. This was quickly done and the Osage were given several hatchets, knives and gunflints. The Osage themselves gave no presents, woefully blaming the poverty of war-trail. But they told the Frenchmen that they would be welcome anytime in the Osage villages. "We have horses to trade," the headman told La Harpe, "And buffalo hides." Indeed, La Harpe was keen to visit these villages. Then theFrench and Osage went their separate ways in the forest.

La Harpe and his company continued their trek through rough mountainous country and camped for the night on the banks of small tributary. They next day, they entered a prairie and continued through it for two days. They crossed a sunken lake and one of the horses foundered, trapped in the muddy bottom. The beast drowned itself seemingly on purpose. The pack saddle was removed and the contents distributed among the other animals. Fantastic herds of deer showed little fear and allowed the travelers to approach them without much cunning. They were killed easily—Du Rivage dispatched one every day with his musket. Wild cattle of the Spanish type were also spied but the long horned bovines bolted from the Frenchmen. Soon, the guides related that the party was approaching the Wichita village. The prairie closed into dense, dark woods and crossing one brook after another with twenty-one horses was a great labor. The creek banks were lined with a labyrinth of tangled vine and sapling trees. In this way, they continued on for two more days, sleeping well at night due to exertion and the pleasant weather.

They encountered the Nabediche camp in early afternoon. The people had already heard of the Frenchmen's advance and were also going to trade at the great Wichita village. Their women were busy smoking a unicorn whose carcass La Harpe examine closely. They were exactly as described by his late friend Monsieur de Bienville—as large as a horse but with a body shaped like a she-goat. The single horn attached at the forehead. And this specimen was exactly where de Bienville had said they could still be found—the headwaters of the Ouachita River. The exotic flesh the savages shared without hesitation and all the Frenchmen found the meat delicious and most memorable.

The Nabediche invited the visitors to camp with them. Tomorrow, they said, we will all enter the Wichita village together and smoke and trade seriously in friendship. La Harpe agreed to this proposition and they camped without anxiety, again well-fed and eager for the morrow.

The next morning, the thirty-first day of their trek, they and the Nabediche cut across a broad, well-worn path through the wooded hills. They followed it to the north until afternoon. Crossing a twisted brook, they found the chief of the Wichita town with six other chiefs awaiting them. The indians were mounted on very fine horses with Spanish accoutrements of silver and twisted leather. The Frenchmen complimented them on the outstanding animals and statements of amity were made by the chiefs. Through the negro interpreter, La Harpe told them, "I represent the Great Chief of France. Who has sent me amongst you to assure you of the protection and friendship he can offer. He can aid you against your enemies, and I, in his name, can complete alliances with you and your people."

The chiefs seemed pleased and brought forth corn meal and smoke meat and a pipe. After exploring these delicacies La Harpe was offered one of the indians' magnificent horses to ride as they all ventured to the village. They rode but a short distance on level ground, crossed another brook, and entered the village.

The Wichita houses were conical grass huts placed close together, stretching east to west. The Wichitas had heard of his visitation and wanted to meet the French representative. La Harpe had heard that other indian peoples were camped nearby. Asking what nations were in attendance La Harpe was told, "Caddo, Waco, Tawakoni." Approaching within musket range of the first huts, LaHarpe was asked to dismount and then two indian men lifted him upon their shoulders. The men began singing and they walked slowly into the village. Men and women left their tasks to join in song and crowd to meet the visitors. Dogs darted about and others sat calmly watching the spectacle.

La Harpe was greatly honored. Four nations, he reckoned, sang to him greetings. They unrolled a buffalo hide outside of an empty hut and sat him down upon it. The hut was for his use, he was informed. The principle indians made a half-circle before him and he gave each of them presents—gunpowder, musket balls, hatchets, knives and bolts of azure cloth. The chiefs showed little emotion and impressed La Harpe with their dignity and decorum. Although some were quite young, they conducted themselves with as much dignity as older chiefs. The Wichita chief was ten years or more younger than La Harpe, and, speaking of his gratitude, he gave the Frenchman a crown of eagle plumes decorated with little buds of all colors. He also received two carved pipes—one was for war and one was for peace he was told. He enquired which one was for which purpose and this was patiently explained to him.

Then, each chief gave a speech, telling La Harpe of their power and the number of scalps they had taken. All of them wished for arms and powder, and welcomed trading with the French. The council went on at great length. Women brought them meat and corn-drink and water and tobacco. La Harpe grew fatigued, but again they picked him up on their shoulders, carried him a distance through the town, and with everyone singing, placed him again on a buffalo robe under brush arbor. As several old men blew smoke upon him a woman came forward and painted his face his face ocean blue. The singing trailed off, and they placed at his feet thirty buffalo hides. Then they presented him with a slave-boy, an Apache he was told, of no more than seven or eight years. The smallest finger on each of the boy's hands was missing, and after thanking the Tawakoni chief for this gift La Harpe asked what had happened to these appendages. The aged chief spoke through the interpreter: tasting his flesh, they had found him unsuitable for cannibalism, but nevertheless the child would be a loyal and useful servant. Again, La Harpe expressed his gratitude. The old Tawakoni replied he regretted that he had only one slave to gift. "Had you been here two moons ago, I would have given you nine of them," he told La Harpe.

La Harpe decided to expend all of his trade goods right then and there, and he ordered everything on the horses to be brought forward. Fifteen hundred pounds of metal powder and cloth was laid out before the chiefs and La Harpe distributed everything among them evenly.

The Frenchmen stayed three more days in the village, lounging and gorging themselves with food and learning more about the people. La Harpe and Du Rivage agreed they were more clever than the tribes of the Mississippi but the fertility of the country had made them lazy. They worked little and spent most of the days eating, playing and smoking. The men were most interested in the European guns and swords, and the women competed with each other as to who could bring the most food to their party. All the indians were greatly interested in La Harpe's two negros. Again and again he was asked if these two could stay behind to live among the indians but La Harpe had to explain that was impossible.

Du Rivage found a post of excellent carving wood and, working with the skill of his youth, he carved on the post the coat-of-arms of the king of France and the name of their company. He added the day and year of their visit and planted it in the middle of the town. When asked what it symbolized, La Harpe told them it was a mark of their alliance and friendship. With some regret, the Frenchmen left the next morning, traveling south to their post on the Red River.

HIGH PLAINS, MAY 1868

Chisholm and Vicente had been hungry before. Many times. But not like this. Their bodies were eating themselves. Their stomachs were dull twisted knots. Nor did they have water. Their veins were collapsing from dehydration. The high plains spring had brought no rainfall for weeks. Creeks were dry. Animals were non-existent. Neither of them spoke aloud about their lack of options. At the end of the day they would have to shoot their mules. The tortured beasts were already stumbling and near death. They would have to drink their blood and eat parts of their hindquarters raw. That would give them two days of life at most. But then they would be on foot on the great prairie. A death sentence. A flock of buzzards circled them lazily in the still blue sky. A pack of emaciated coyotes followed them, smiling at their misfortune.

The mules plodded forward, their riders silent with regret. This was supposed to be a simple contract job, one of dozens of similar missions they had embarked on over the past thirty years. Two little girls had been taken captive from a far western Texas ranch, their parents and brothers murdered, mutilated by the girl's Comanche captors. The girls' uncle had reached out to Jesse Chisholm. The man had gold, silver, horses, cattle, rifles galore—and he would trade mightily for the girls' return. Chisholm had accepted the job and his partner, Vicente, had of course come along as well. Vicente had once been a Comanche captive himself. Chisholm had traded two blooded mares for him when he was but a child in 1844.

Chisholm was well-known as a trader and emissary and man of plains. Although Cherokee by clan, he lived and married among the Creeks. But eight months a year he was on the prairie. He wore a Comanche Peace Medal around his neck, the likes of which no one had ever seen. It gave Chisholm carte blanche among the Comanche clans to come and go freely. But now, thoughts of their reputation were forgotten. The silver conchos they carried in their saddlebags as trade stuffs were a useless mockery. It had been a very dry year. And they were dying.

There was no sound except that of hooves stamping heavily into earth. Then Vicente turned to the older Cherokee man, almost was he smiling. "Do you smell that Uncle?" He asked.

It took great energy for Chisholm to even speak, "What is it?"

Vicente grinned, "A huckleberry fire. And it is well-concealed."

They both knew what that meant—Comanche. Chisholm took a deep breath. They might live after all. He scanned the horizon and saw nothing. "Where?" He asked, twitching his nose.

"It's drifting, Uncle. They will find us."

It was Yampahreekuh-clan Comanche who found them, small boys on malnourished glassy-eyed ponies. Buffalo Hump's people. They said the men were out hunting and had been gone for days. There were no animals to kill.

Chisholm and Vicente followed them slowly to their camp. There, the women recognized them at a distance and began to wail. The men dismounted and the Comanche women crowded around them, their faces dirty their bodies covered in worn buckskin. The Thighs, Buffalo Hump's eldest wife took Chisholm's arm. "Why are you here Brother?" She asked, "We are starving and you will only die with us."

Chisholm answered her in perfectly inflected Comanche, "We came to trade for two little girls your people took from the Tejanos. They were taken on the Salt Fork of the Red River."

The Thighs nodded and Chisholm continued. "I talked to Buffalo Hump's oldest nephew a full moon ago and he said they were with you. We cut your sign twelve days ago. But then we ran out of food. And water."

The Thighs kept her face blank. "They were cotton-headed girls," She said, "Very strong. They would have made good women. But when we ran out of food, my husband threw them away on the prairie." The Thighs shrugged and made a motion as if she were tossing a pinch of salt.

Chisholm hung his head and felt bile rising in his throat. It was all for nothing. The were going to die out here for no reason at all. The girls were already coyote dung. He looked at Vicente and saw the light dim in his eyes. Wasted, he thought, after all these years we are wasted. "Come sit with us in the shade Brother," The

Thighs took his arm. "We have a few drinks of water and tobacco. That is all we can share with you."

They sat in a nook of isolated hackberry trees and smoked their pipes. Chisholm and Vicente each took a cup full of brackish water and held it in their mouths for long minutes before they swallowed. "I am glad my husband is not here to see you find us in this condition," The Thighs confessed. "He would be very embarrassed. He is an old buck for sure but he can still lose his temper very quickly and dangerously"

"We all know the prairie very well. But it is a bad year to be moving. The worst I have ever seen." Chisholm shook his head. "I would tell him this and he would know I spoke the truth. With one cup of water you have already helped us more today than we can help you."

"One of our grandsons killed a young black bear six days ago. It was quite a feat, really. He killed it with two arrows. That is all we have had in a long time. Some of the bear's fat remains. You could cut up pieces of soft leather and mix it with the bear fat and eat it. We have all done this. There is perhaps enough left for two men."

Chisholm looked at Vicente and the men nodded at each other. "That would be appreciated," Vicente said and The Thighs roughly ordered her youngest sister-wife to prepare them this indelicacy. Chisholm turned to Vicente and lowering his voice spoke in Spanish, "Vicente, you know this is my seventieth summer."

"Yes, Uncle."

"I'm nearly at the end of my days anyway. Take all this bear fat for yourself. It may be too late for me."

"No." Vicente shook his head. "Never. We've been through too much for that. If we die, we die here together, with these indians."

Chisholm looked at him for a long time and felt tears streaming down his cheeks. "OK," he said.

The woman brought them the bear fat and leather and they ate it in one fist-sized chunk. As soon as the fat hit their stomachs the revulsion rose and they both knew— the bear fat had soured. A Comanche could eat it and keep it down. But they could not—they stumbled out of the camp retching and sunk to their knees to vomit over and over. Vicente's eyes lost focus and he collapsed like a dead-drunk as the women rushed to help them.

Vicente opened his eyes and saw the endless blue sky obscured by hackberry branches and leaves. They had dragged them into the shade to die. He heard squalls of delight and whoops of joy. Laughing and melodic Comanche language filled his head like a pipe dream. "The men are returning!" he heard, "They have meat and water!" He rolled over and leaned on one elbow and saw them. Ponies full of meat wrapped in pronghorn hide and bison bladders and gourds full of water on pack animals. "We are two days from fresh water!" he heard Buffalo Hump shouting, "We will make it!"

He sat up and turned to where Chisholm lay beside him. He touched the man's arm. "Wake up, Uncle," he said, his mouth sandpaper rough and dry but Jesse did not move. Vicente saw that he was not breathing. He put his hand to his mouth. Chisholm was dead. Vicente shuddered and Buffalo Hump hurried to the side of his old friend and trading partner. Buffalo Hump dropped to his knees next to Chisholm's corpse and screamed like a wild cat. He pulled at his hair wildly and two dreadlocked clumps tore loose from his skull. The Thighs ran to his side and he pushed her away, end over end she rolled. Whipping a knife into his hand, Buffalo Hump slashed his forearm deeply over and over and then fell prostrate, weeping.

The next morning, a stone-faced and wounded Buffalo Hump squatted next to Vicente and offered him his pipe. Vicente took it and puffed gently. "How would Chisholm want his body prepared?" Buffalo Hump asked, "In the white man's way or in the indian way?"

Still numb and barely cognizant, Vicente could only shrug. "I don't think he would care," he replied, "He was Cherokee. They are as much white as indian."

Buffalo Hump nodded. "OK. I will have the women do it our way. And we will make sure that you live to go to his people and tell them his fate.

Photo by Jyl Johnson

James Murray is a farmer, writer, and historian living in Cherokee County, Oklahoma. With Murv Jacob and Deborah L. Duvall, Murray co-wrote *Secret History of the Cherokees* which won the 2012 Best Historical Novel Award from Native Writers' Circle of the Americas. He has also published writing in *Counterpunch* and *Race Traitor*. Murray is currently working on a novel about Cherokee outlaw Ned Christie and another set in contemporary Tulsa, Oklahoma.

www.ingramcontent.com/pod-product-compliance
Lightning Source LLC
Chambersburg PA
CBHW020658260626
47157CB00008B/3083